BEAT GIRL

Beat Girl

BONNIE GOLIGHTLY

Includes a rare author profile and interview

"Bonnie Golightly: Author Still Living in the Shadow of Her Name" by Wendi Watts is reprinted with permission from *The Daily News Journal*, Sunday, August 30, 1998, © Wendi Watts – USA TODAY NETWORK via Imagn Images.

This edition of *Beat Girl* is published by Giant Books, which reissues overlooked works by women writers. GiantBooks.org.

ISBN: 978-1-965751-17-6

Bonnie Golightly:
Author Still Living in the Shadow of Her Name
By Wendi Watts

Bonnie Golightly might have remained an enigma of Murfreesboro's past, but for a conversation at The Woman's Club last winter that set the memories of her in motion again.

While chatting at a December meeting of The Woman's Club, a member who had not grown up here commented on the number of literary connections in the community…Charles Egbert Craddock [pen name of Mary Noailles Murfree], Andrew Nelson Lytle, Andre Norton, Will Allen Dromgoole…

And a native of the city asked, "Have you heard of Truman Capote?"

"Yes, but what's the connection to Murfreesboro?" the newcomer naively asked.

'That Capote Thing'

The main character in Capote's short book "Breakfast at Tiffany's," which was turned into a movie starring Audrey Hepburn, may have been modeled on a woman who grew up in Murfreesboro.

The character, Holly Golightly, bears some striking similarities to the real woman, Bonnie Golightly.

The daughter of an MTSU professor of education, Bonnie grew up in the shadow of the university's campus from the mid-1920s to the mid-'40s. She went to dances and parties and was regularly mentioned in *The Daily News Journal's* Partyline column.

Until recently, most of "the crowd" who used to hang out at the Golightly house at 1212 East Main St.—Susan Bragg, Kacky Holden, Charlotte Dill, Frances Nelson—thought Bonnie was dead. Others weren't sure. A few thought she was probably alive somewhere living as only Bonnie could.

To later generations, tales of her youth in Murfreesboro and later life in New York have been regarded as containing a grain of truth and a large measure folklore.

But Bonnie is very real and very much alive.

And she may forever be defined and, much to her chagrin, remembered mostly by one event that brought her national attention—what she refers to as "that Capote thing."

During World War II, Bonnie and her husband, Bob Sheffield, moved to Greenwich Village, where Bonnie owned and operated a bookstore called The Park Book Shop. She later divorced Sheffield but continued living and working in the city.

At the same time, Truman Capote was living in New York and making a name for himself as a writer. Among his most famous works set in that era is the novella *Breakfast at Tiffany's*.

Holly Golightly was the story's main character, a charming 19-year-old cat lover with an aversion to attachments of any kind—a wild thing not meant to be held down by social conventions.

Holly's fictional life and Bonnie's real one shared many similarities—growing up in the South, living in a brownstone on Manhattan's East Side with a bar around the corner on Lexington, singing folk music, having an assortment of dramatic and theatrical friends and acquaintances and having a love of cats.

"I knew an awful lot of people who knew Capote," Bonnie said in a recent telephone interview from her home in New Haven, Conn. "I did not know Capote at all, and he denied all of his life that he had based the book on me. After he died…somebody admitted in *New York Magazine* that he had based the whole thing on me."

Capote "knew somebody who knew me very well, a bitch, who really bitched the hell out of me," the 79-year-old recalled. "She was somebody who, she thought she had taken away my boyfriend. My boyfriend returned to me and she really had it in for me from then on. And I got backlash for years, *years*. She apparently talked to Capote and Capote didn't know I still lived in New York or anything else, and he thought he was perfectly safe in using my name.

"I first heard about this from a friend, David Lubis, also a writer—a published writer—who lived in an apartment I had lived in a few months before.

"Christmastime came and I dropped by the apartment to see if I'd gotten any mail and he said, 'Oh, I didn't know you existed!' And I said, 'What do you mean?' And he told me he had heard Capote read from a work in progress…and the name [of the main character] had been Connie Golightly. 'Connie,' for constantly traveling.

"And so I said, 'I'm not going to put up with this,' and called up Hiram Haydn…somebody I knew at Random House [publishing company], and said, 'Please don't let Capote use my name.'"

Bonnie was told the name "Golightly" had been used before in literature and was not unheard of as the name of a character.

"But…from what I had been told about the work in progress, there were too many similar things," Bonnie explained. "I just didn't want it. And I especially didn't want it because I was a writer myself and I didn't want him to use my name.

"So Hiram went to Capote, who agreed to change the name, and the name was changed to 'Holly Golightly,'" Bonnie said, and added with more than a tinge of sarcasm in her voice, "Big deal."

Breakfast at Tiffany's was published by Random House in 1958 and appeared in *Esquire* magazine the same year.

Bonnie was so outraged, she filed libel and invasion of

privacy lawsuits asking for $800,000 against Capote, *Esquire* and Random House, according to an article in *Time* magazine.

The *Time* article appeared in the Feb. 9, 1959, issue and said, Capote "claims that his Holly had three 'counterparts in reality,' none of them Bonnie. 'One of them is dead—she died in Africa, the other two are very much alive and have no intention of suing me.'"

Capote also is quoted in response to Bonnie's lawsuit as saying, "I have never met nor seen this lady…. It's ridiculous for her to claim she is my Holly."

Capote never publicly revealed whom he based the character of Holly Golightly on, but a number of women who knew the author have seen themselves in her. Author Doris Lilly, novelist Pati Hill, artist Beatrice Whistler [Dabney] and actress Carol Grace all claim to have been his inspiration, according to information posted on an Internet site about *Breakfast at Tiffany's.*

But Bonnie claims she paid a high price for Capote's work because she shared her last name with his character.

"It really semi-ruined my writing life," Bonnie says. "I'm not kidding you…. I was advised by publishers to change my name. I had become a figment of [Capote's] imagination…. It was very discouraging, first of all. It made me feel as if I were a bird that had its wings pulled off…. Afterward, I didn't write very much on my own. I wrote mostly things that editors would come to me and ask me to write for them."

Bonnie's lawyer dropped the lawsuit.

The Capote incident is still a thorn in Bonnie's side, and she continues to fight to have her writing and contributions to the body of American literature recognized, contributions her friends from childhood had no doubt Bonnie would make.

Memories of Murfreesboro

Born June 23, 1919, in Chicago to Thomas J. and Emily Rogers Golightly, Bonnie was their second child. Her brother, Thomas Jr., was seven years older.

When Bonnie was an infant, the family moved to North Dakota.

In 1925, the family moved to Murfreesboro, where her father joined the faculty at Middle Tennessee Normal College. Bonnie began her formal education at Campus School in what is now known as Kirksey Old Main on the MTSU campus.

Among her first-grade classmates was Susan Lytle, now the wife of John Bragg, retired state representative.

"I knew her all the way through school," Susan recalled. "She wrote quite a bit. I can remember her sitting in class and not paying a bit of attention because she was writing short stories. And she was good…. Even in grade school, she came and did what she wanted. I guess that's what made her different.

"She was very independent. She had a good mind, but she didn't care about school at all," Susan continued. "I can still see her in English class with a tablet just writing up a storm…. She had no discipline. If she liked you, she was a friend. She could tell you off if she wanted to."

Even as a child, Bonnie knew she wanted to be a writer.

"Everybody in my family wrote," she recalled. "I started writing when I was 8 years old. I wrote stories…things about playmates. You know, silly little things."

After completing grammar school at Campus, Bonnie attended Central High School.

During these years, the Golightly home was the regular meeting place for Bonnie's friends and acquaintances.

"I had an awful lot of friends in Murfreesboro," Bonnie said. "We had a 'crowd' as we called it. There were about 10 of us in the crowd. Susan was one of them. Emily Crichlow, Juanita Highman… We'd meet after school, largely, and then at night, too, on weekends. We always had parties on weekends, very often at my house…. I don't know why it was…. I had my own car when I was 14, a Willys-Knight roadster with a rumble seat, apple green. Very cute car."

One of the reasons the Golightly house was such a popular spot was that Bonnie's parents were more permissive than most in Murfreesboro at that time, members of the crowd explained.

"The [Golightly] household was not quite run like anyone else's in Murfreesboro," Susan said. "There were no restrictions."

"The gang seemed to go to her house on Friday nights," recalled Charlotte Dill, another member of the crowd. "I guess we liked to go there because Bonnie wouldn't let her mother and daddy bother us."

But all of Bonnie's memories of growing up in Murfreesboro are not happy.

"They used to say that it had 10,000 people," Bonnie said. "Actually, there were 7,900. Everybody knew everybody. I mean, there were people one simply did not know. You knew their names; that was it. It was a very snobby place. It was just awfully snobby. When the Cotillion Club was formed, a lot of really nice people got blackballed for no good reason. Meanness.

"My parents were older than my friends' parents, so my parents did not socialize with my friends' parents, so it made sort of a gap. But I was never top drawer really. I was secret top drawer…. It was a complicated thing."

Bonnie did not want to stay in Murfreesboro. She didn't know where she wanted to go, but she did know what she wanted to do.

Since she was a child, Bonnie longed to be a writer.

"Our house was right on the edge of town in those days," Bonnie said. "The city limits were about a half mile away from 1212 E. Main St. And I used to sit on the front steps and think, 'I really don't want to go North, but look at all those interesting cars going by…. I really don't want to stay here, but I don't want to go North.'"

Experiences in Literature

North, though, is where she ended up when she married Bob Sheffield, one of her father's students at the university. Bob had grown up in New York and Connecticut.

The couple moved to New York, where Bonnie opened

and operated Park Book Shop from 1943-48. The shop specialized in out-of-print and rare editions.

From 1949-53, she was assistant manager at Hacker Art Books at Hacker Art Gallery.

Since 1954, she has been a freelance writer and editor, currently working as an editor with *Writer's Digest*.

"I knew an awful lot of people, but I didn't know them well," she explained. "I'm one of those people who can name drop and name roll, but that's about it. I didn't have close associations with most of them…. [Poet and author] William Carlos Williams was the only one I knew very, very well in that group. I met an awful lot of his friends too. But I knew him quite well.

"He was living in Rutherford, N.J., at the time. But he came into New York frequently as people do in New Jersey and Connecticut. They come into the city for one reason or another. And I met him because I had read something called *In the Money*. He wrote three novels, and that's one of them. And I wrote him a fan letter. He came by the shop and was fascinated. So, we became friends, and he and Josie, his wife, invited me to their house by the bay, and I would go out there frequently. And William game me copies of all his books.

Bonnie became an author in her own right. She has penned 20 books, including novels, mysteries, gothic fantasies and romances. She also did novelizations of movies such as *Legend of the Lost*, *The High Cost of Loving*, and *Olympia* for Avon book publishers.

During her writing career, she has used the pen names Milton Rogers, her maternal grandfather's name, and Helen

Sheffield.

Her most successful books have been *Shades of Evil*, a mystery, and *The Wild One*, a novel about an upper-class teenager who falls in and out of love with an older man.

Her first novel was based on a memory of Murfreesboro.

"The first novel I wrote was about…an incident down in the bottoms [in Murfreesboro]." Bonnie said. "I don't know if you still call it the bottoms or not, near the river. Poor people lived there.

"And there was a little boy who had a wolf on a chain, and I saw this wolf. We used to drive around all the time. It's one of the things we'd do…and I'd see this wolf on this chain and that was the basis of my first novel, which nearly got published."

Her favorite work is the last one published, titled *Polly Paris*, a gothic tale now out of print.

"I wrote eight books before I ever got published," Bonnie said. "I didn't get published until the early '50s. And I never would have gotten published, I suppose, except for having connections. That's the only way you really get ahead in this damn business…. I had a friend who worked for Avon books, and she commissioned the first book."

Among the books she wrote for Avon are *Beat Girl*, *The Intimate Ones* and *The Integration of Maybelle Brown*.

The last book she wrote, *The Veil of Order*, was about memories of Murfreesboro. It remains unpublished.

"I wrote that for myself," Bonnie said. "It nearly got published countless times. And it got to the point an editor would call and say, 'Let's have lunch,' and I'd say, 'Are you going to publish my book?' They'd say, 'Let's talk about it.' And I'd say, 'No thank you,' because at least 20 times that happened."

The 1,200-page book "was about Murfreesboro and made-up stuff about the South…. It's really not about Murfreesboro per se. There was nobody in it identifiable. But it was an amalgam. It was a saga opening in the late 19th century and went up to 1946, I think, something like that. There were similarities to people I knew."

Bonnie produces her work on a typewriter and never revises.

"I sit down and I write until I drop," Bonnie explained. "The longest I think I ever wrote without really stopping except to get up and answer the phone or open a can of soup was 125 pages."

That was a 12-hour write-a-thon.

She has the plots for her stories in her head.

"And then, the voices talk to me and tell me what to say, I've always said," Bonnie said. "It's a ridiculous kind of way to characterize it, but that's pretty much the truth…. But I simply cannot revise. I have tried, and I ruin it every time I try."

When inspiration strikes, she usually starts writing immediately.

"If I get interrupted, it's usually forever," Bonnie said. "The long book, *The Veil of Order*, I got interrupted and it took me, I think, a couple of years before I finally finished it. It just died on the vine."

She added that writers have their own preferences in how they create their work.

"Writing is such an individual thing that you can hardly characterize that it should be this way or that way or the other way," she said. "It's whatever way it comes out. That's the best advice to give any writer."

Her days now are filled with reading, writing and taking care of the six cats who share her home in New Haven—three inside, three out.

What does she plan to write in the future?

"I don't know," Bonnie replied. "I guess, I just…thought I had something to say, and one of the reasons I don't write much anymore is that I don't have anything to say."

*

Maybe so.

But her old chums at Murfreesboro's Woman's Club, where Bonnie's mother was once a member, have plenty to say about their friendships with Bonnie Golightly. And they are certain the book will never close on their memories of the wild young girl who will always live in the shadow of her name.

BEAT GIRL

Chapter One

The night before my mother died of cancer of the liver, she got roaring drunk. "One last time," she said (and downing all of those martinis was really heroic in her condition). "Just one last time before I'm catered by the Frank E. Campbell people."

"Oh, *Mother!*" sobbed Joyce, my brother Bart's wife, and went careening out of the room, looking like a drunken circus tent in her mother-to-be clothes.

"I'm sorry she gets so upset," my mother said, really meaning it, "but why does she insist on calling me 'Mother'? She's got a perfectly good one of her own. Or at least adequate," she amended, for she and Ida Bradford had never been friends.

"Oh, Mother," Bart said quietly, repeating Joyce's very admonition, except on him it was something else. Bart understood Mother, probably better than anybody—including me—unless you count Tennie, our maid-cook, who had been with Mother and Mother's family all of her life.

That night Tennie was there too. We were in Mother's bedroom. Mother had insisted she and Jess come in for a drink. And when Joyce swept out on her tidal wave of tears,

Jess looked embarrassed, as he always did, and Tennie looked fierce.

"You got no call to carry on this way, Miss You!" Tennie spoke out, her eyes flashing.

"Stop calling me that, you black wretch!" Mother said, and Tennie looked madder than ever.

It wasn't that Mother had race prejudice, or that she didn't love Tennie and appreciate her—maybe even more than she ever loved anybody else—but Tennie had picked up the habit, in the past few very difficult months, of calling Mother what she always called people she didn't consider "quality folks": Miss You, or Mister You, on the pretense that she couldn't remember their names.

"Stop all this," Bart ordered sharply. Then he went out to find Joycie, and nurse her back to peace of mind.

After he had gone, we were all silent and morose. Jess looked miserable. He has very dark skin, but that night it was more gray than black, and he looked as if he were dying, along with Mother. And I guess he and Tennie too both sort of thought it was the end for them. I know I felt it was the end for me.

"Here, Miss Cornelia," Tennie said gently, as she went over to the bed and plumped up Mother's pillows. Then she quietly took her martini glass away from her. "You best get your rest."

"R.S.V.P.," Mother murmured languidly, drunkenly, sleepy, dying. "Or is it something else?" She looked at me.

I wouldn't say it, but Jess did. "It's R.I.P., Miss Cornelia," he told her, his voice husky with dammed-up tears.

I don't know whether she heard him or not, but she made a small gesture with her hand, and, with a little sigh, turned over on her side, facing the wall, her hand still lying where she had dropped it, like a small discarded fan. Such a pretty little hand. It had been a size 4½ (French glove size) when she married my father, so she had said. And now it wasn't much more. It was smaller than my own. I picked it up, placed my palm against hers.

"Darling," she said faintly. But she didn't turn around. And after a while, after Tennie and Jess had tiptoed from the room, I tiptoed from the room, tears gushing out of my eyes like the hot waters of Old Faithful. That was all. She died in the night.

They wouldn't let me or Joycie go to the funeral because Joycie was so *enceinte* and I was so young. But those weren't the only reasons, for Joyce was still ambulatory and I was seventeen. Actually, both of us were too broken up—I, in my private way, and Joyce in her public one. Had Joyce liked Mother much, that chestful of histrionics she unloaded on everybody would have made healthy sense, but it was so patently a combination of great-acting, guilt, and self-pity on her part that it drove grief right back inside me and bottled it up to ferment, so that I couldn't even cry about anything else, much less Mother, for ages. Further, when I saw the exhibition Joyce put on, I had to force myself to speak. I guess Bart and Tennie and Jess thought I'd been stricken with lockjaw or had gone into Catatonia, that state with the prettiest name. Anyway, their cure for me was to keep me from the funeral and hustle me off on a plane for England the next day, to stay with my Aunt Maude, as had been more or less arranged previously when Mother first found out she was going to die.

Now I wish I had forced them to let me go to the funeral. Had I gone, perhaps I would not have renewed my Holy Grail-type search for the Beautiful People. For when Mother died, I felt that the only one of the Beautiful People I knew had died too. That's why I couldn't talk. Who could I talk to? All the same, I was determined to find someone; you can't live inside a bottle forever. But this, like most searches, led to a lot of trouble along the way.

When I say that the family, or what there was left of it, put me on the plane, I mean it literally. Joycie and Bart were in full command, very much the senior partners that day, and I was a very minor one, will-less, choice-less and next to speechless. But they were quite sanguine about that, and waved me off with heartiness and hope, thinking, no doubt, that if the roar of the plane didn't bring me to, the roar of the British Lion would. I wasn't so hopeful; I knew how much I had lost and how deep I would have to go to retrieve it. More than six feet up or down.

They, of course, were counting on my fondness for my Aunt Maude and her fondness for me. As a child, I had thought of her as a sort of goddess or queen. It was she who had taken me all over Europe, watched over me most of the years between seven and twelve, had been at close call when I was in school in France, and Switzerland. But most important of all, she had been the embodiment of my dead father whom I had never seen, she being his only sister. I can remember how I used to gaze at her sometimes, when she let me sit in her dressing room as she combed her long hair before the vanity mirror, and I thought how heavenly beautiful she was. But once back in England, I soon realized the mirror had the right word for it: vanity. She wasn't beautiful at all, but she was vain.

It must be a terrible thing to be a fallen angel, and I'm afraid it was in my face, the gladness draining out, almost upon seeing her again. In the first place, naturally, she had grown old—quite old—as she was much older than my mother. And she had settled down into thinking of herself as an English Lady, her American girlhood being so far in the past. The lovely waxen features I had once thought of as so beautiful had now coarsened with time, as if the wax had melted and had begun to run. Had I been capable of objectivity at the time, I would still have seen her beauty, but all I saw was a vain old woman who looked at me with cold disappointment. You see, she, too, I now realize, was confronting the vestige of a broken image. Her little chubby baby with the lovely ash-blonde curls and bright eyes had been swallowed by the present me: a dark-haired, neurotic wraith, underweight, funereally dressed, with dark circles under its eyes.

Considering our immediately mutual letdown, I suppose we did reasonably well together for the next long months. But I did not warm to her or my surroundings. More and more England seemed to me rather like a cold forbidding governess—all iron-gray stern and tight-lipped—and I thought my feet would never be warm again.

On the surface, poor Aunt Maudie knocked herself out. She immediately put me in a "best" school full of frightful females with sick-looking teeth way out in front; and when the "season" started the Teeth crew and I moved into town and took our places at the deb "dos" and were admired and talked about. I was also in that last group of debutantes who were presented to the Queen, a fact that floored one and all except me. As I say, I was dead and cold. Even in the summer my feet were cold.

Another thing, Aunt Maude and I found we had simply nothing in common. She had become as thoroughly English as T.S. Eliot, and simply doted on her "town house" and its treasures. (Town house was actually an awful old apartment with ceilings as high as a Norman church and countless drafty, heatless rooms hung with tapestries.) I once remarked to Aunt Maude that it reminded me very much of an ancient castle—a most witless thing to say, for she immediately divined with her astute eyes that I felt trapped, an imprisoned princess held in the tower. But she said nothing, which was her way.

However, what she did not know was that the "castle" gave me the horrors for other reasons. It was more like a boot camp for necrophiliacs than a home for quiet, mending me. Everything about it spoke of the dead, from the priceless hoardings to the private ones of private value; most especially the latter. I was haunted, for instance, by most of Aunt Maude's cherished private heirlooms brought over from Virginia when she was a bride. There were baby shoes circa 1800; there was a ghoulish vomit-making thing under glass which looked exactly like flowers spun from varicolored thin wire. I would have continued in my innocence had I not one day admired it, as it hung in its ornate oval frame, and been told that great aunt so-and-so had artistically woven the hairs of her dead sisters, grandmother, and great-grandmother to form this tender memorial.

But the Longtree relics were not the worst: there was the matter of Aunt Maude's deceased husband, Uncle Philip— Sir Uncle Philip—dead before I was born, but almost as alive. She had preserved everything from crumbled slippers (why all this foot fetish among the Longtrees? Was it inherited?) to hookah, mustache cup and scissors. No fingernail clippings, though, but again locks of hair. And everywhere you looked, his likeness. In the library, of course, it was a painting of him in full military regalia, while elsewhere there were simply old-fashioned photographs, also always showing him in uniform. He was such an army man that I am sure he not only never missed a campaign, war, or skirmish in his time, but I doubt seriously if people were even able to quarrel without him. One picture I had particularly liked when I was ten, and still a great soft-hearted admirer of Aunt Maude's personal trag-edies and treasures, was labeled "Sir Philip in the Boxer Re-bellion." I had gazed at it with real affection, for at that time Bart had had a fine champion boxer which used to take prizes at dog shows, and I had thought that kindly, pug-nosed Sir Uncle Philip had been the very man who had understood boxers and their puppies and had reasoned them out of their fights. I was under no such illusion now. For me the place was peopled by "he-haunts" and "she-haunts" as Tennie used to call ghosts, and Aunt Maude, with her austere eye and powdery thin skin, rapidly crumbling into dust, was at once their custodian, soon to join them, and my relic. I had enough relics. One primarily I kept in my heart and head and could not forget: Mother.

Constantly I thought of Mother. She was with me in the drawing room, the W. C., the scullery, the ballroom, the schoolroom, and my room in the apartment. And never as she was but always as she had been that last night with her face turned to the wall, like a picture, her pretty hand left behind in discard, behind her once lush and then wasted eighty-five pound body, and her voice hovering over her body like a visible wisp of fog saying, "Darling." My Darling Death. She was my own private ghost. Aunt Maude had hers, and I had mine—only I was even more selfish than Aunt Maude: not only would I not give her up, I wouldn't share her. In all those months, I never spoke of her at all.

Aunt Maude's discretion was as impeccable as her vanity, and, since she had better things to do than pry into the secret grievings of my adolescent heart, she decided to go right on with the pleasures of her life. The chief of these was "The Nobility."

Transplanted to England through marriage at an early age, she had, like a gently lovely but wild rose, taken to the soil. Over the years, and doubtless with Uncle Philip's help, she had espaliered herself over everything British, crawling carefully year by year up the trellis until she had reached the pinnacle, covering all. By all, I really mean all. She embraced and thrived on everything English with a rich full growth. I suppose she expected to start the same process in me—a slip of a girl, as it were. At the age of seven, yes; at forty-seven, perhaps; but at seventeen, no. Especially my sort of seventeen.

She trotted out endless younger sons, Honorable Miss So-Forths, lads who had come into their titles early, and ladies of title no bigger than Goya's "Infanta," but for me they were not the Beautiful People.

It took Aunt Maude a year and a half, thousands of pounds of English money, and a heart-shaped lifetime of shattered daydreams to realize that though I might be her heir I'd never be her idealized heiress. And when I went to her, braced for argument and strong truth, and announced I was going back to America, all she said was, "Oh, dear." It was then I knew she was a really wise woman.

For though I am fairly sure Aunt Maude did not know why I had failed her, I am sure she had accepted the fact that I had, and that was quite enough.

Chapter Two

The day he called me was the day I began to plan to tell Aunt Maude. His voice over the telephone was enough in itself to creak open the door of Aunt Maude's mausoleum, but then as we spoke that door blew wide open and let in AIR. Air! Fresh, clean American air. And I realized I had been breathing antique, lifeless dust. It was Pritchard Allyn, sort of a member of the old crew in New York, en route home after a summer in Europe. Oddly enough, he was the first of my old friends who had called me, though I knew from home that others had sometimes passed through.

I was cagey as hell at first, putting on my very best British accent, and sounding as aloof as a duchess, even though Pritch was the first man I had "known"—carnally, that is. But then he hadn't been more than a promise of a man. I wondered if he had grown up.

"How about tea?" I asked him after the preliminaries, dropping my accent back into its slightly English cradle where it normally resided these days.

In answer he suggested dinner, saying he had "things to do."

"Very well," I said, hoping I sounded indifferent rather

than put out, and we named a time; he would pick me up here.

Aunt Maude asked me if he were anything important, and, quite innocently, I asked her what she meant. Important was one thing to her and another to me. Which was she talking about?

"I mean, is he someone your—brother approves of?"

"I suppose," I said listlessly, for I had never thought of Pritch or any of them in terms like that. What was my brother's approval? In America, it meant he liked the same people I liked; here, to Aunt Maude, it undoubtedly meant that Bart was the head of the house and must *approve* my friends if I were to see them, whether he cared to associate with them or not.

"In that case," said Aunt Maude, "I'm sure the young man will dress for dinner."

It was merely a suggestion, of course. But then, Aunt Maude, being so English, never made anything stronger. I dressed for dinner.

I climbed into the first thing I saw and swished around the drawing room waiting for my "American young man." Aunt Maude had had other plans for her evening, and was, I think, glad that something had turned up to take me off the servants' hands. Even if it was *only an American*. The italics are hers, even if she wouldn't claim them.

The dress I wore was right for England and the time of year, even if it was wrong for America at any time of year. Aunt Maude's dressmaker had done it, and she is what I can only describe as a dewy-eyed dowdy genius, completely in tune with her time, her town, and her tot of gin. Seldom sober and probably unable to focus her bad eyes on anything smaller than a billboard, she somehow convinced Aunt Maude that she was always "up" on everything; that she worked with Captain Molyneux hand-in-secret-glove and you couldn't go wrong with her at half-the-price. At first, I protested with American-type vigor, but I was soon hushed—by the hush—and gave in. What did it matter, I felt, if I looked like…? Name it, you can have it. Anyway, I wore one of her copied original creations that night—my "late summer dinner gown"—as conservative and serviceable as an English walking shoe. Made to last too. As I say, Aunt Maude had resigned herself to me forever.

But that was where Pritch came in. Just as I heard the bell, I methodically checked his arrival on the Ormolu clock (something I would not have done at home except for a Mr. Right, had there been one). And as I heard Cecil, Aunt Maude's butler, admitting him, using that funny intonation on him which as good as said: "*You*, sir, are an *American*," I knew all at once what a hideosity that clock was (if it had been human it would have been strangled at birth), what a fatuous snob Cecil was, how glad it made me that Aunt Maude was out—way out—and how glad I was that Pritch was *in*. My mausoleum door was creaking.

"Baby!" In he walked handsome in his handsome dinner clothes, and held his two arms out to me like an invitation to a seat in a garden swing. I took them. He kissed me soundly on both cheeks.

"You look like a *great lady*!" he exclaimed. "All grown-up, dignified. Like a member of Parliament!"

Cecil, I noticed, heard all this, and, with a smirk hidden behind his decorum, inquired if we would be wanting "cock-tails." The hyphen was his.

I turned to Pritch, who said, "Why not?"

And Cecil went to fetch cock-tails, a concoction, I assured Pritch in his absence, that would be memorable, if not drinkable. But Pritch had suddenly interested himself in Aunt Maude's house.

His back facing me, hands in trouser pockets, he studied one of her cherished Constable landscapes while I studied him. I had seen her Constable often for the last months, but I hadn't seen him.

Yes, I decided; whether or not I had changed, he certainly had. No longer the too-tall, almost wavering silver birchtree-blond-sapling, he was now an adult plant—whatever that meant. And I wondered what it did. I couldn't remember. Pritch was foggy, as foggy as the time we had "made out," as we said in New York, when I was a virgin, and had clung to him with all the fire, passion and hate of a circus animal that night near Montauk. He had taken my virginity. But nothing else.

So now he was new to me. And old at the same time. No birchtree stripling. He was a man. How old I didn't know, but a man. I remembered he had been in Harvard in those days. By now he must be out—way out, from the way he looked. For now I saw he was not tall at all. He was going to be one of those men about whom one said: yes, he should have been tall, you can see it in the authority in his glance, the way his eyes are steady and colorless, the expression on his face.

And, as if just for proof, he turned and said, "This is a fabulous house!" It was a statement of discovery, as if I were a Dresden doll which simply belonged in the collection, on some chimney piece or other.

Cecil brought the drinks—Martinis, I think. I drank mine, and Pritch held his. He continued marching around, looking, looking.

How long can one stare at the back of one's dinner escort—especially if one is hungry? I said as much.

He turned, and a knife went through me as the lamplight made familiar all those familiar features I'd forgotten: American, but so Pritch Allyn that he became a nation, a country in himself. I had forgotten his cheek was so golden.

"I guess you still spend a lot of time swimming, and at the beach," I murmured.

He took some of his drink. "Beach? I haven't seen any sun this summer, except through cathedral or plane or train windows."

I took a sip of my drink. "Did you do the Chateaux Country?"

He nodded, then he took my hand, led me to the couch and began to talk about his summer.

"I don't know if you want to hear," he said, boyish again, in spite of the serious and direct look of his once blue eyes, now angry sea-gray, "but I've been taking Europe in—in the Grand Tour manner."

Then he told me how he was lost, drifting, didn't know

what he wanted to be—poet, architect, pianist, painter—and how he doubted his talent in all. During this, his hand had circled my arm closer and closer, like an ever tightening bracelet. The things I felt because of his touch were like explosions in the distance. But I knew they could come closer. And if they did, I could short-circuit. I had once before.

I stood up. "Aunt Maude would love you for loving her house."

"She must be a great Aunt Maude," he declared, and continued his tour around, admiring this piece of glass, that painting, that chair, and stepping around her Aubusson carpet as if he were afraid he would tread on someone's face. I said this, and added that all these things of hers were in everyday use, that she wanted them "lived with."

"But not lived up," he corrected me suddenly. "I'm glad you live in such a house."

And that's when he discovered the Sheraton table—Aunt Maude's pride and joy, since there were chances it was an original—the first and last.

I thought he'd never stop about it; his eyes were full of love for it—enviably so—as if the thing were human, and female. That's when I suggested dinner, and quick about it. I really was hungry.

In the taxi (and I didn't know where we were going), he still sat like a man surfeited, replete. I had to ask him to give the driver directions before his reverie was broken. "I certainly want to meet your Aunt Maude," was the answer to that, echoed by, "I certainly do, Chloe. I certainly do."

I promised him he'd meet her, wondering what she

would make of this particular kind of enthusiast. But it wasn't my business, and how did I know that it wasn't just another creative crush he'd got into? I heard him give the driver the restaurant address. If it wasn't the Ritz, at least it was food, whether I'd been there or not.

But riding along in a taxi with Pritch, an American, I felt awfully sophisticated, well-informed: after all, I did know the places to go for drinks, dinner, dancing, and just to be to-gether—and he hadn't asked me. How grim and square, I thought. And let's have a grim, square evening. Something to take home. And be proud of, Babbitt-proud-of a la the '20s. In a way, we were the '20s, all of us. Only I felt more on the Evelyn Waugh line than the Sinclair Lewis. Maybe I was wrong. Maybe I was rebellious Carol from *Main Street*. But one thing was certain: Pritch was a Babbitt, albeit a young one and slightly less Rotary Club and more couth. But every-thing about him screamed American. That his sights were ra-ther higher was in a way pathetic, for somehow I felt he would never make it. I wondered what he was doing with his life besides gnawing at culture, and even as I asked him I was just sure he would say he had already been taken into his father's firm.

"Me? I'm taking post-graduate work at Columbia next year," he said.

Which just proved that my insights were scarcely 20-20. "In what?" I asked, and his answer was so detailed and com-plicated that I still didn't quite know—but he was studying something that had to do with art history and restoration of art treasures; the latter explanation is what hung me up. But no wonder he was such an enthusiastic bore about Aunt Maude's house!

Now that I had him started on the culture theme he didn't seem to want to stop. He went on and on about periods, museums, private collections, galleries in New York and London and God knows what all. How could he have thought I was really interested? Finally he said, jokingly (I hope), "Why, Chloe Longtree, I'd sell your soul to the Devil to own a Tiepolo right now!"

"Why pick on me?" I answered. "Anyway, I'll buy you one instead. It's cheaper."

"I don't know about that," he said. "Tiepolos fetch fancy prices, if and when one comes up for sale. In the world auction record, their price-range history starts at—"

"—A million dollars?" I broke in.

He stared at me. "Are you serious? Of course not." Then he stared again. "You mean you're loaded?"

I nodded, and he gave a low whistle of surprise. "Good J.C.!" he exclaimed. "I always knew you had a few bucks, put you down for a few hundred thou, but—You mean you got real cash? Straight arrow?"

"Straight arrow. I've got bread. By the bankfuls."

"Gee, kid." He was looking at me strangely now. "Gee."

"I don't like those new eyes you're using on me," I told him only half joking, for I'd had about as many lean and hungry looks in the past few months as I could stand.

"Where'd you get it? You mean your old lady left you all that loot?"

That did it. Without so much as a clap of thunder, I had

a veritable cloudburst of tears. I sobbed and sobbed and sobbed. I drenched my own handkerchief, his, my petticoat, my evening coat, and even my hair.

When I could speak again, I was hoarse and said all my t's and d's as if I had a cold, and found myself saying them against his lapel, since he had, quite naturally, taken me in his arms for succor. "I haven't talked about Mother since she died," I started to explain, but found myself ending up on a wail.

"Gee, kid, I'm sorry. I didn't know. Look at me, Chloe. I didn't know, I didn't know."

He rocked me in his arms, and after a while it had the desired effect, and I stopped mourning.

Maybe I *really* stopped mourning, or at least shifted into second-gear mourning, for we then discussed quite calmly all my bad blue months in England and what to do about them. The mausoleum door was wide open now, and I was outside.

We talked freely about our parents, aired all our thoughts on the matter. Pritch, it seemed, had plenty of sibling as well as filial problems. All of his brothers and sisters—three boys and a girl—were older by far, and his parents were so old they practically went back to the Stone Age: sixty-five each.

"They're as old as Aunt Maude," I exclaimed, impressed and sympathetic.

"They live in a place rather like hers too," he told me. "Only they don't have any taste. The only good things in the place belonged to their ancestors."

"Oh, a lot of the stuff of Aunt Maude's are hand-me-downs too," I told him to make him feel better, even though it wasn't precisely true; her best things she had bought herself. Then I asked: "They don't live on the upper West Side by any chance?"

He nodded morosely, considering, I guess, that this was another strike against them.

"I'm sure I know where they live. Is it terribly grand, a huge old fortress-type of apartment house built back when apartment houses were a rarity?"

"Yes. You know the place." He named it. "Rather than terribly grand, it's grandly terrible. At least I think."

I didn't at all, and said so. As a matter of fact, it was one of my favorite places in New York, architectural atrocity or not. All of the apartments in it, so I was told, were simply enormous, ceilings so high you could only see the top on clear days, etc. And, since the place had been built for the very rich and the very chic of the period, the first who thought it unstylish to continue living in their tremendous old houses, the architect of the building had included in an effort to pamper these spoiled people a horse-and-carriage-size elevator which could bring milady's equipage up to her very door, so that the only effort she had to expend was that of opening her flat door and being handed in to her carriage by her footman.

"Those heaven days," I sighed.

"You think so. I wouldn't live there again for anything."

"I would," I sighed again. "I've only been there once—" (I didn't tell him it was to visit some people my mother considered déclassé but was sorry for in their straitened circumstances) "—but it was marvelous."

He looked at me rather sharply. "It strikes me as odd, in that case," he said coolly, "that you dislike your aunt's place so much."

I gave him a perceptive and admiring look. "Touché," I said. "Very touché. You've given me something to think about."

Chapter Three

We hadn't really passed the soup course before I knew that this was no ordinary dinner and that this was no ordinary date. Pritch made me have a new respect for Babbitt-type young men—if that's what he was in the least. He was fun, and yet he was sound at the same time. And he had good intuition, as well as artistic intuition—or sensitivity, as most people are content to define it. I liked him tremendously. So much so that I was thinking of ringing up Aunt Maude and making some excuse to stay out overnight, which, of course, was a little precipitate on my part, because we had only been brotherly and sisterly so far in our embraces, but I had that definite feeling.

Also, one of the things I had learned since I left most of my baby-skin, is when and when not to be the horizontal woman—or whether the choice will come up. I had been, lately, completely upright morally, if these things really are part of morality, but not so at first. I had thought sex was a way out of mental misery and grief, a mistake as universally prevalent as syphilis, and went to bed with so many men I met that I practically forgot the meaning of the word vertical.

But that time was long since passed, and therefore, considering that Pritch was my first physical "love," not only was there the initial attraction, but fastly accumulating was a real stockpile of energetic sexual desire, because I found him so desirable in the mind and spirit as well as elsewhere.

I knew something was going on with him too. His eyes had softened and yet brightened at the same time: like a sea, formerly gray, when a streak of sunlight hits it from a crack in the clouds.

Because of this, we began paying elaborate compliments to each other—or entered "the courting stage," as it is known. Our rapport was established, and the time for intimacies would soon be at hand.

Needless to say, I was terribly excited, and I could tell Pritch was too. He said some wonderful things to me—about me—and I listened to them as if the words were as fresh to me as my feelings were, as if no one had ever used them or heard them before. He told me how attracted he was to me, told me how pretty I was, how mature, how intelligent, how et cetera. The language of love.

But, as so often happens in affairs between people who have known each other a long time in too many other lives and relationships, the well-padded brickbat department was as irresistible as the hearts-and-flowers. The fact that we both had clay feet *had* to be pointed out, I suppose, and past private opinions, of a critical nature, had to be aired, in order to clear the air, so to speak. Or at least Pritch obviously thought so.

He started first, and the opening words weren't out of his

mouth before I knew I had not steeled myself enough for the probings and insinuations that were to come: the well-tempered clavier was going to make some ill-tempered music when her turn came. What he said was:

"Clo, you know you're a funny girl. The last time I saw you you seemed so mixed up. Not stupid, but goofed up—running wild, like a car without a driver, because you couldn't make it with your mother dying."

I felt my cheeks heat up, and knew I had turned pink. He was after nothing short of my Achilles' heel. How bold and cruel. "Oh?" I said in an aloof voice. "Is that the way you thought of me?"

"Sure. Everybody did." His smile was still warm and intimate, casually disarming. He didn't know he had already gone far too far. "Getting engaged to that guy three times your age," he continued, "and then breaking it up was *crazy* crazy stuff. I guess it didn't bother you too much, but it really threw him. And the rest of us, too."

"That's very interesting," I replied. "Funny nobody mentioned it to me. I suppose all of you thought I should have gone back to Charles and gone through with it?"

"Lord, no, Clo. But the fact that you started it in the first place proved you were like a runaway. But, as I say, you've stopped now. You've really changed. What made you stop?"

"Gravity," I said, my humor still in need of restoration.

"Good sense, I'd say," he further mollified.

But I was feeling very unreconstructible. "Do you mean you and Avery and all the crew really thought I'd permanently flipped?"

"Sort of," he admitted. "But you haven't. I guess some of them have flipped instead."

I didn't want to change the subject from me to them. "Do you understand, Pritch, what my mother was really like? What she was as a person, aside from being my mother?"

Pritch thought about it, and looked rather uneasy as he did so. Then he came up with: "I didn't know your mother very well. Anyway, let's not argue."

"Let's not," I returned. "But since we've gone this far, and since you're the first person I've been able to talk with at all about Mother, I…I think I should tell you a few things."

And so I told him; tried to explain about the Beautiful People; how I'd felt when I knew she was going to die, then trying to hang onto myself all those months until she did die—like falling, falling deep down in a well; and when I hit bottom all the sense and life and air was jolted out of me, and I just closed up in a vacuum.

"But you're not in a vacuum now, Chloe," he assured me facilely.

"You didn't let me finish," I said. "I was going to say that when the air was knocked out of me grief poured in, and *then* I closed up. So grief was still there, fermenting. And I was simply a bottle. With an airtight stopper in it."

"But you're all right now, aren't you, kid?"

I looked at his beaming face with a very cold one. "No, I'm not really all right. I'm just better." I would not give him the satisfaction of hearing me add: since you came. And anyway, I wasn't sure that he himself had not put the stopper back in the bottle again. I suddenly felt very alone, and wanted to be actually alone.

He continued to grin at me in that self-satisfied and somehow intimate way. Clearly, he did not know how deeply I was offended, else he would not have strolled on toward the quagmire with such a confident spirit: "You ought to come back home," he advised me lightly. "Stay with Joycie and Bart. You should see their kid. That would cheer you up."

"Ugh," I said. "How repellent."

"What? Don't you like kids?"

"It has nothing to do with 'kids'," I said acidly. "I suppose you don't know how Joycie treated my mother, or how she behaved—"

"She was very upset, I know."

"Yeah," I agreed. "Very."

"Don't be that way, Chloe," he said after a time of studying me with now serious, worried-looking eyes. "You should know I'm—well, I knew you before I knew them."

"I suppose you're dear friends with Joyce and Bart now?" I asked. "And they've sent you as an emissary, is that it?"

"Don't get hot about it," he answered evenly. "I am friendly with them, but they didn't even know I was planning to see you. I got your address on my own. Don't you see, Chloe, I wanted to see you. And now I am genuinely concerned because you seem unhappy. I think you should get out of England and go someplace to work things out."

"And you think that place is New York? Certainly not. I wouldn't dream of living with Joycie and Bart and their baby."

"Maybe you and one of your friends from school or something—?"

I shook my head adamantly. "I'm going to stick it out here. I've got to, or nothing will ever work."

"Is it that desperate? You sounded so calm and—"

"It isn't desperate at all, really."

He gazed at me in a way that made me very uncomfortable. "Why is it that you *seem* so close to making it, look so much like you are—?"

I shook my head, feeling as if everything were blurred and melted out of recognition, as if I were going blind. "Let's talk about you," I said tightly.

"We don't have to. You understand me. It's you neither of us understands."

"Words, words, words," I said, really feeling in the dark now, for of course he was right: my motivations were as unknown and curious to me as new germs under a scientist's microscope. But I lacked the scientific curiosity—and courage—to track them down.

I guess Pritch divined this and found my stubbornness both stupid and disgusting. I could almost feel his warmth recede from me, and the light of interest fade from his eyes. Now, he was studying me coldly. "Want to go?" he asked, standing up before I'd even had a chance to nod.

In the taxi there was no doubt about it: he had given the driver my aunt's address; he was taking me home, getting me off his hands. I felt the tingling numbness that always comes when I've made a great and admitted defection; I felt unspeakably sad.

All I could think of was regret, regret that I had fouled this up so entirely that I was being peremptorily dumped. Now we would not go to bed together after all. He would escort me to the door, say goodnight, and that would be that. And in a few days he would be gone. As a matter of fact, he was gone already. All that remained was his duty to deposit me where he had found me. No more phone calls, no more anything. He had had it. The mausoleum door was closing again, with me back inside....

I sat stiffly in my corner, knowing I simply appeared silent and hoping I appeared casually silent, not the frozen and hurt thing I had become. I wondered if he was wondering about the thoughts touring around in my mind. Of course he wasn't. He had lost interest, and I knew it.

Without turning my head, I took stock of him out of the corner of my eye. He was a study in placid indifference. God knows what he was thinking—cathedrals, art, New York. Whatever it was, he had certainly parted company with me, as surely as if we had been riding in separate taxis. It made me furious, but glummer than ever. I felt like something evil, a poisonous snake on the way to the taxidermist's, or disease—gray, horrible cancer—something to get rid of as soon as possible, before I became dangerous.

I'm as bad as you think me, I started to say, but just then I startled myself considerably: tears were simply pouring out of my eyes, scalding hot and uncontrollable. I had pride though, at least; enough to want to keep my tears to myself. If he saw them, all right, but they weren't for him anyway. They were for me. I didn't want his sympathy; I wanted my own. What had I done, what was I doing to myself anyway?

We had stopped in front of Aunt Maude's, and it took me a few minutes to realize he was paying off the driver, that he would not be keeping the cab. He helped me out, took my elbow lightly and we went up the steps.

Cecil let us into the flat, and I averted my face when I returned his good evening. I certainly didn't want to share my tears with him. He told me my aunt had just come in, and I nodded, ducking my head down.

"Great!" I heard Pritch exclaim, and then he wheeled me around eagerly. "Do you think it's too late to disturb her?" He was so excited by the prospect of meeting my aunt that I don't think he even noticed my tears. Dying for a chance to talk about his crush on the 19th century.

I glared at him. What a colossal nerve he had! I started to blurt out at him that these were the first words he had spoken since dinner, then I thought, what's the use? I had already parted with enough of my shabby dignity. "I'm sure she'd like to meet you," I said. "You two have a lot in common."

He missed the irony, of course, and just at that moment Aunt Maude came out of the library saying: "How pleasant, Chloe! Your friend from the States." She had both hands outstretched.

Chapter Four

They got on like a pair of identical twins, just as I had expected. Her delight was unbounded: such an *appreciative* young man, even if he was an American! I watched the two of them racing about, inspecting everything like a couple of appraisers, and was filled with absolute loathing.

Aunt Maude's British accent was getting thicker and thicker, and Pritch's deference was getting so deferential that I was afraid he'd be on his knees to her in one more minute. So in the midst of this glittering spectacle, this shining performance, I thought I had best extinguish my own small light and creep silently to bed. I tried a preliminary goodnight on them, and they didn't even hear me.

This left me in a peculiar position: should I simply leave? No, that was a childish, pouting way to do things. And after all, if I felt left out, it was my own fault. The best thing to do was ignore them too. With that, I rose and poured myself another glass of sherry; I'd dedicate my attention to that.

They had disappeared into the dining room now; Aunt Maude wanted him to see the Romneys. When they did that room, she would have to do the drawing room—even though he had seen it earlier—and God knows what other cells. Well, if that's what he wanted. No use in having his entire evening spoiled. I decided to be good-natured about it. Did my decision have anything to do with what happened? I don't think so. I think Pritch had had it in his mind all along, all the time I had been having my feather-fight with my own neuroses.

Because what happened was that when he had had enough of his grand household tour, he simply came up to me and said, "Ready to go dancing now?" as if that was what we had planned all along.

Aunt Maude beamed at us as we left. "Have a good time, children," she said, and I knew that I had won her full approval for the first time since my arrival. And through absolutely no fault of my own.

I looked up at Pritch in pure delight when we got outside and said, "Where are we going?"

"Where do you think?" he answered, handing me into the cab that had just stopped for us.

I was just on the point of saying I didn't know, when suddenly I did, for he took me in his arms without a word. Then he gave the driver the address of his hotel.

Going up in the lift I felt as if I could have accomplished the trip under my own power. Joy is as much a physical sensation as a mental one, and I tingled all over with it, feeling as disturbed and excited as an embryo two minutes away from birth.

And it was like that all the way. We walked in his room and he didn't even bother with the light switch, but simply put me back in his arms as if that was the only place I was ever made to be.

I had remembered Pritch as another kind of lover. That night so long ago at Montauk he had been fierce, and we had made love like ravenous wild animals. Now his passion was slow and measured, yet I could feel the strength of it when he kissed me. It was not the ardor of pure desire this time; it was the ardor of love as well.

Gently I felt him unfastening my clothes; he paused every now and then to kiss me. When the undressing ritual was finally completed, he picked me up as carefully as a flower and took me to bed.

Again and again we made love—love that was swiftly and completely satisfying to both of us. And yet before he had moved away I would feel myself desperately wanting him again, and even before I could touch him, to let him know, I would feel his arms around me again, and the sharp deep cry of desire would break from his lips even as it did from mine. And again we would be plunged into that endless silent world of brilliant ecstasy where so few lovers can ever really go.

At last this craving need subsided to some degree and we lay there in warm bliss and love exhaustion—no other fatigue like it. But I knew I couldn't go on lying there in the dark secret heaven I had found in his bed. Insatiety probably would never leave me, but all the same I had to leave it. I made a move to get up, even as I felt his arms tighten around me once more.

"There's always tomorrow," I whispered.

"Stay!" he urged me.

For a moment I gave in, but dimly, a long time back, I remembered having heard Big Ben strike two or three; much too late even then, and now it was even later. Quickly I slipped out of the bed, eluding his arm, and stood beside him, feeling almost irresistibly drawn to return.

In the half-light from the open window I saw his arm reach for me. "Tomorrow," I whispered again, and went to the chair where he had put my things.

My hands trembled as I dressed, then I saw the bedside light go on, and felt his look before I saw it.

I turned. He was sitting up in bed, completely naked, looking at me in the most curious way. It struck me that his expression was somehow alarmingly out of contrast with his nakedness. It was almost the calculating look of an executive giving a job applicant the once-over and should have been accompanied by a fully-clothed body in a business suit.

The smile of happiness which I suppose had been perched on my lips like a silly bird on a branch, simply flew away, and again I turned my back—coolly, I hoped—and continued to dress, taking my time, buttoning each button, getting all the snaps. I hoped he didn't see how much my hands were shaking. Now I fiercely did not want him to know how deeply moved I had been by his love-making.

"You want some help with that zipper in the back?" he asked at last.

"No, thanks," I said with equal lightness. "It doesn't matter whether I get it or not. I have my evening coat."

"Suppose your aunt is waiting up for you."

"She isn't in the habit of so doing, nor," I added with regrettable sharpness, "does she help me undress at night."

"Still no sense in going home half-dressed," he said.

Giving him an angry look, I tugged at the zipper, knowing its tricks full well, knowing it would have defied an acrobat to handle it alone. Then suddenly his hands, cool and efficient, were on me, and the zipper shot easily up making its soft buzzing sound in transit.

"There," he said, but he didn't take his hands away. One slowly caressed my neck, and the other curled softly over my arm as it was something he owned and prized.

"I have to go," I stammered, close to tears, not at all understanding him now, a few minutes before—or, truthfully, at all, ever.

"So do I," he said gently. "In the morning. Somehow I didn't get around to telling you earlier."

I guess I staggered slightly from the impact of this news. No wonder he had behaved as he had. "But darling," I cried. "Must you—must you?"

"Reservation's made. Flying TWA."

I simply couldn't believe it. It had been so short. And for what? Why couldn't he cancel it? Everybody missed planes. I was just about to blurt this obvious suggestion out when he cut me short.

"And there's something else," he said quietly, looking into my eyes, his hand still on my arm. "This isn't just any old flight I'm taking. I'm late as it is…."

Late? My mind jumped ahead like a hurrying crippled animal, desperate for a way out, an explanation. If it was a job, something like that…*anything*…it couldn't be so important as tonight and… Then suddenly I knew. "Who is she?" I asked, my mouth feeling frozen, as if it could barely open to form the words. "Somebody I know, I guess…."

"Yes, it's Joycie's sister—Les—Lesley."

"Oh," I murmured like Dumb Dora. The whole situation had about it something so familiar, so odiously familiar…. And then I remembered: the night before Joyce and Bart's wedding, down at the foot of the stairs at the Bradfords' when I had seen Pritch for the first time since he'd shelved me…if you can call it that after only a few dates…when he had told me he was there on account of Lesley; that yes, they were very good friends indeed—something of the sort. And I had thought of the color green as it was in one of Mother's paint tubes. Green for jealousy. I could almost smell it now—oily, horrid. "When is it?" I whispered.

"Wedding's the end of October. Lots of parties and things," he gestured, looking almost at ease again, so glad he apparently was to have got it all out in the open. "I thought you knew."

"No," I shook my head, truly dazed now, and feeling the exhaustion from what now proved to be our wasted reunion absolutely overwhelm me. "No," I said again, feeling something more had to be offered. "Joycie never writes since the baby. Occasionally Bart does, and they telephone whenever they both get tight and sentimental. But I guess we've kind of drifted apart—" I said no more. There was no room just that instant for anything more than the huge lump in my throat.

"Chloe…"

I looked at him wretchedly, angrily. If he asked me to forgive him, or asked if I was sorry I'd—

I guess he saw what I was thinking, for the appealing look and voice changed. "I'm not sorry. I love you very much. Also, I'm counting on you...."

"Okay, okay!" I said hotly. "Let's leave it at that, shall we?" Abruptly I stepped back from him.

"You'll never get a taxi at this hour," he said, his voice as calm and smooth as glass. "Let me get dressed, and I'll walk you home."

"It's miles," I told him, knowing my own voice and face were unpleasant and full of contempt. "You've forgotten how spread out London is." Anything to hurt him.

"How will you get home?"

"I'll call Aunt Maude. She can send the car for me."

"At this hour? Won't she be horrified?"

"Heavens no!" I laughed like a wild thing. "She's used to it. I stay out like this all the time."

"Come on," he said firmly. "You and I are walking you home. We have things to talk about."

I wanted to yell: I DOUBT IT! But what was the good? Maybe he did have things to get off his chest. I'd gone this far; listening to him wouldn't change it one way or the other.

It was cold outside; another London winter already promised in something in the early fall air. I hadn't looked at him since we left the hotel, and now I didn't either. I dipped my face down into the collar of my white satin coat, glad I had worn it after all.

"Do you want to go to Lyons' for some coffee or something?"

"No," I said.

"You aren't going to talk to me, I see," he remarked after a time.

"That's right," I told him, still not raising my head.

"You know what I wish?" he said, trying again. When I didn't answer, he said, "I wish you'd come to New York."

"For the wedding?" I asked sarcastically, unable to resist this much at least.

"No. For your own good."

"Suppose you leave my own good to me."

"You know, of course, that I'm going to tell Bart and Joyce that you're not happy here."

"And are you going to tell them why?" I blazed at him.

"No," he said. "But only because I don't know."

I stopped and confronted him in the dimly-lit street. Of all the gall, mitigated or unmitigated! Then my rage fell limp. Of course he was right—he didn't know why. Nor did I, really. I couldn't blame my state of general discontent on him. He accounted for only a few hours of it, as compared with many months. "Don't tell them," I said quietly. "It won't do any good. I'm not going to go back to New York."

He gazed at me in that sad, resigned way wise but weak parents do at incorrigibly wayward children, and we resumed our walk, as silent as before.

We were in the heart of the London night—or rather past it, and in the cold, depressing region of the early morning when all of it seems like a historical ruin, a monument rather than a living city. The breeze didn't help either. As it ruffled my hair it only made me feel more unreal. An unreality moving in the interior of another unreality. Two figures from the past, ancient—timeless—moving in the limitless plains of the past. And so we were. Pritch and I had been here before, walking along the Good-bye Road, which, for us, was indistinguishable from its parallel thoroughfare, Hello. "—'a tale told by an idiot, full of sound and fury—'" I murmured to myself.

"Are you quoting something?" he asked.

"No," I lied, yearning desperately never to have to lie again, yearning desperately for him to say he loved me, as he had back there in his room; wanting to ask if Lesley were prettier, smarter, more fun than I—wanting the world.

Chapter Five

After that ghastly and ghostly walk, the waters of boredom, complacency, and day-to-day piecemeal peace settled
back over everything as if Pritch had never been there for
those few terrible and yet wonderful hours. I had my custom-
ary feeling of vague but unidentified discontent with my life,
except for the always-present dark angel of my mother's
death, and a sharper cognizance of my real distaste for my
aunt. But neither of these two things was strong enough to
make me think, as I had that night, of making a change. And,
as usually happens, I met Somebody.

Somebody was an awfully nice guy, but he reminded me
too much after a while of all the other awfully nice guys, and
I knew I just wouldn't be able to stand it. But awfully nice
guys don't require dramatic endings to their love affairs, and
I was in no hurry to let him down. He would appreciate the
slow, easy, painless way, and that was what I was giving him.

He was a sports car enthusiast, and had a terrific custom-
built job—a Lagonda. We used to take wild, fast trips all over
the English countryside, the only dashing thing about him
being his car and his driving. Sometimes, to tell the truth, he
scared me out of my American wits. Anyway, I'd never get

used to left hand traffic and high speeds on such Lilliputian roads.

One day we had driven up to Windsor for luncheon, and that was the day—perforce—I made up my mind. I got sick as hell and barfed like a dog all over everything, including the car upholstery and my new fall Balenciaga.

He was terribly sympathetic, mopped me up, and talked at interminable length about how everyone got car-sick at one time or another, but I knew I wasn't car-sick: I was afflicted with a slight touch of pregnancy. So that night I told Aunt Maude I was going back to New York, and that's when she said, "Oh, dear."

That was exactly a month after Pritch had gone. And though I knew that I could kid myself another two weeks or so, sooner or later I'd have to face it—and, if I wasn't careful, big as life. I'd made no close girl friends in England, and certainly none who weren't "nice"—*i.e.,* ignorant in the matters where my current interest lay. I had to get back to New York and see Avery. If ever a girl lived who would know about abortions, she was the one.

Aunt Maude thoughtfully cabled Bart my plane schedule, but outside that did not interfere. And before I knew it, I was off.

Whenever I travel—especially when I fly—it seems as if my mind deliberately shuffles through all of its available material and comes up with a selection for contemplation during the trip—this in spite of the fact that I, consciously, always take along a lot of books and magazines. The books and magazines always stay right in my lap, unread, and my mind takes off, almost from the minute the plane leaves the ground, and goes its own way—usually detailed, sometimes devious, and always complicated. I knew this time it had decided on My Problem.

All during the flight as I gazed down almost unseeingly at the tiny white-capped ocean waves, I was thinking: why did you let yourself get pregnant? What good will going back do? He'll be married in two weeks. Why didn't you just go lose yourself in Paris? They have lots of doctors in Paris. Or why not have his child? It won't ruin your life—only middle-class people let such wonderful acts of nature ruin their lives. How nice to have a child all your own! You'd grow up to-gether, go everywhere, be independent. How do you know you are pregnant? The questionnaire continued. The usual sign plus car-sickness is melodramatically insufficient. And it isn't enough that you've just had that certain feeling all along, ever since it happened. You are a masochist and a fool, just dying to suffer.

By the time we arrived in New York, I felt dead tired from thinking, and had concluded that I was behaving like a fool. Yet why shouldn't I go back to New York, pregnant or not? And looking up Avery to be on the safe side was not an act of further folly.

I suppose the only thing I didn't ask myself was whether or not Pritch was in love with me, and the reason I didn't ask it was because I knew. Pritch was strongly attracted to me, yes, but he didn't love me—he would be slow and cautious about falling in love. And I had even come to the conclusion that the chances were he didn't love anybody, including his fiancée, Lesley. In all likelihood, this marriage was simply the pleasant outcome of "the right thing to do." He had never written me a line after he left London, and actually, I had not expected it—only hoped. Certainly as we came into Idlewild that day, it never crossed my mind to look him up in New York or involve him in my life in any way.

And that's how with all my cold, brilliant thinking and working things out, I got the surprise of my life.

I think I saw them and knew it was them the minute the plane touched the runway, even though they were specks standing with other specks beside a faraway dollhouse-size air terminal.

So when I unfolded myself and gathered up all my unread reading matter, my airplane kit-bag, my purse, my papers, my hat, I did not dare to look outside the plane's door on past the landing strip to where all the meeters stood pressed against the fenced gates beaming rather idiotically in the direction of the meetees, debarking one by one. I did not dare, but somehow it just happened anyway, and there they were lined up in a straight line, cheery as anything, waving and shouting something: Joycie, Bart, Pritch and Lesley.

I think it was my guardian angel who delivered me into their tender, excited and noisy care, for I am sure I could not have simply walked.

Naturally, they were all over me at once, Lesley as enthusiastic as anybody, and we, like most of the other groups around, were a scramble of embracing arms, rather like excited octopuses, everyone talking at once as shrilly and as fast as possible. Or almost everybody. I was like a dead center, the eye of a cyclone, and simply did not protest against the kisses on my cheek (Pritch's were cool and soft as damask—like roses) or who took my arm, and who took the other, and who took them away. I was propelled through brief customs, now borne along by other European travelers rather than my own group who stood aside, beaming again even more radiantly than before, their eagerness in no way abated.

As I waited for my turn with the customs people, I snatched at the thoughts that crowded my mind. But they all raced by like fast-moving clouds on a windy day. Everything was blurred, too fast, too fast….

Then I was with them again, and each was clamoring for something different: Joycie was trying to tell me about her baby, a boy named Cornelius after my mother—an honor my mother would have questioned, as I knew she detested the name. And Bart was trying to find out about Aunt Maude and the mysterious reasons for my sudden return, and both Pritch and Lesley were jabbering about people we all knew and all kinds of frantic parties. Then it occurred to me, quietly, just like that, that they were all really hysterical. Why?

Bart and Joycie had a new car, I saw. They had sold Mother's big one and had bought a perfectly frightful but roomy chrome-covered station wagon. "We bought a house in Connecticut," Bart explained, starting the car.

"Didn't we tell you?" Joycie said. "Oh, Daddy, I know we told her. It's near Mother and Dad," she turned back to me. "Small, but just right for us for the present. We were up there all summer, and we're going every week-end this fall if we can, or until the weather gets too bad."

"Mother loves having them so close," Lesley said, her eyes bright and full of friendship. "And she's simply frantic to see you. My God, Pritch. Look at her!" She exclaimed.

Then they all looked at me and noted my various changes in visage, coiffure, weight, color and attire. I felt very young, and wondered if I made them feel very old. I also felt very lonesome. There wasn't enough togetherness to go around.

"Where are Jess and Tennie?" I asked.

"Oh, they're fine," Joyce assured me, tossing her black long hair slightly to get it out of her way. I had forgotten this gesture. I had forgotten a lot. It seemed incredible to me that Joycie and I had been such close friends all through childhood, and that even understanding, not to mention friendship, had come to such an abrupt stop when she married my brother. Now she was like someone I'd never known, like the daughter of a dear friend long dead who had inherited some heartbreakingly familiar traits and mannerisms of her deceased parent. The truth was that looking at her again after a year and a half, all of my resentment came back. This, plus Lesley and Pritch whom I regarded as gingerly as if I had been seated between two tins of TNT, boded no good for America and me either. Where to go next? I thought. The world, even mine, which by rights should be large at my age, was becoming a very cramped place.

Then I noticed the back of Bart's neck. I knew him so well, and for so long, that even after not having seen him for ages, I knew instinctively he was very uncomfortable, mentally uncomfortable, about something.

He spoke slowly, "Joyce, you haven't answered Chloe's

question." That proved it was not pleasant, for he had been calling me "Mole" before—his old nickname for me.

"Haven't I, dear?" Joyce said in serene innocence. And I thought, how vile!

"No," I spoke up. "I asked where Jess and Tennie are."

"Oh, did you? I thought you said 'how.'" She gave a slight cough.

"They aren't with us anymore," Bart said rather flatly. "Joyce felt they would be happier in Baltimore."

"Baltimore!" I exclaimed. "Why they haven't lived in Baltimore for years! They've always been with us. Haven't they, Bart?"

"Oh, come now, Chloe," Joycie said, giving me a smooth smile with just the tiniest bit of jagged edge to her tone. "They've always gone down there to visit. And they really weren't happy here. Things weren't the same after Mother died."

I felt a tight little wad of anger in my throat, threatening to choke me or make me explode. So that was the pitch. Bart had as good as said so: Joycie had fired them.

I still pride myself on the fact that I didn't say a word.

Joycie pitched merrily into the chilly silence like a health swimmer attacking the waves on a December day. She, too, pretended to love it. She splashed and capered, and I didn't listen to one word she said.

Vaguely, I knew she was being joined in her conversational romp by her sister. And morosely, feeling really apart now, except for the knowledge that somehow Bart was still with me in spirit even if he couldn't be in actuality because of his wife, I waited for Pritch to get in on all this small-talk fest. But he was as silent as I. I looked at his profile: neither sad nor glad. It told me no more than a silhouette.

Lesley was sitting on the edge of her seat telling Joyce the latest sick joke, though Joyce begged her to stop, that she didn't get them and she thought they were awful, even when tediously explained. I found myself listening; I did get them and right at the moment sick jokes seemed particularly apt. That's why I didn't hear what Pritch said—anyway, he almost whispered it.

I turned to him. "What?"

"I said I've got to see you by yourself. Have lunch with me tomorrow."

"No," I said quietly, but firmly. "I'm sorry."

"Please!" His tone was as keen as a knife.

"Go ahead," I suddenly heard Lesley say. She had turned around and was staring at me full face. Her expression was impossible to decode. Only something defiant and hurt in her eyes tipped me off. "I know all about it," she told me steadily. "And I wish you would have lunch together."

Chapter Six

We went to "21" and we made the most minute of talk
and were very gay about old times, how we all used to come
there together—Avery Stafford, Tim Atkins, he and I.
Though actually I think we were all together there only once,
and then he and I had not been together: that had been my
Tim Atkins period. But the headwaiter I was glad to see still
recognized me, as he always had because of Mother. And the
food was divine.

Funny how sometimes when you are upset the most,
your appetite is heartiest—like the condemned man's last
supper. We had that marvelous chicken soup with curry in it,
heart of palms, and an entree.

I chattered all through the food without knowing I was
chattering. It was like being cold and not knowing it. We
made all kinds of inane comparisons about English food and
French food, and even compared notes on our stays
abroad—I had gotten to France twice and Belgium once
while I was there—and we found out we had not only stayed
in the same hotel in Belgium, but that we had had rooms on
the same floor. At different times, of course. But that's how
the conversation ran—scampered. In London we had talked

only of ourselves; here, at home, we talked only of selves other than our real ones. And it was all so easy, so pleasant. Right up until the time that I realized what was happening. And again I got that sunk feeling, the same I'd had in London that night after dinner when he was taking me home. This was another—and harder—"never-again." For this time there was good reason. Number one: his marriage; number two: my interesting and top-secret condition.

I was suddenly so full of agony that I thought I was going to be sick. I guess Pritch saw how wan I'd become.

"What's the matter?" he asked starting up in concern. "Don't you feel well?"

I shook my head. No use in being brave if I couldn't hide it. "Too much real food after that English famine," I said.

He helped me up, quickly got the check, and helped me outside. I stood on the sidewalk on Fifty-Second Street and coaxed myself into recovery. He stood by, saying nothing, looking worried, watching me as I fought it out.

"I'm all right now," I finally said.

"You want to go home?"

"No," I said decisively, which wasn't hard. "Home" was a strange place indeed these days. Joycie and Bart had also failed to tell me they had converted the two lower floors into a duplex, retaining the upper two for a duplex for themselves. Of course it was *their* house, according to the will….Mother had left me the equivalent in stocks, and the furniture and things were to be "equally divided" at some future mutually satisfactory date. But I didn't like it at all.

"Feel like walking then? Or a drink? We could go to the

Plaza."

"No," I told him. "Why don't we look up somebody?"

"Who did you have in mind?" he said with a slight frown.

I started to suggest Avery, because Avery was so much on my mind just then, but he said instead, "Let's go to my place, Chloe. I really did want to see just you, by yourself."

"So you said," I returned coolly, trying to seem poised and unconcerned. But my heart leaped up all the same, just as if he had whistled to it.

We took a taxi, and I inquired in my controlled mild tone if this were his own apartment he was taking me to.

"Yes," he said. "I can't bear living with Older Generation up there in that massive rockpile."

"Do you have lots of room?" I asked. "I mean, is it going to be big enough, or will you move?" I didn't add, after the wedding, for it seemed to me tactfully implicit in the question.

"Quite big enough," he answered, scowling slightly as if he were mad at the back of the cabdriver's head.

I said no more, but noted we were headed downtown toward the Village. Somehow I had never thought of Pritch as the Village type. He was far too elegant, too fastidious and, admit it, something of a snob. Still, snobs lived in the Village. Probably the biggest ones. I observed and remarked upon the number of new buildings which were going up everywhere, and quite justifiably Pritch had no comment to make on this. He was in another of his silences, apparently a gloomy one. What was he thinking, this guy who waxed hot and then cold? Whatever it was, I loved him so. But I put this thought gently out of my mind, like an extravagant bit of something admired in a shop which common sense told me not to have.

"You really don't care much for Joyce anymore, do you?" he asked in a troubled voice.

Why shouldn't I tell him the truth? "No," I said coldly. "I don't."

"Joyce feels bad about it."

"No, she doesn't," I answered. "She thinks she should, but she doesn't. She wants it this way. She made it this way almost singlehanded. She's what Tennie used to call 'contrary'—she wants to hang on to that cake she's eaten. She won't ever change now."

"You mean she wants to be big grownup sister-in-law, in joint command with big brother, and at the same time play dolls with you on rainy days, or when the juvenile mood suits her?"

"Something like that."

"I thought so, but I promised her I'd speak to you."

"Oh, so *that's* what you wanted," I said. Now I felt fully deflated. But that was nonsense. What else could he have wanted?

"Partially," he said in his noncommittal way.

"Is it about Lesley too?"

"Naturally, it concerns Lesley too."

That, I thought, was the zenith in the enigmatic, or else it was as obvious as a fire engine in a busy street. Probably the latter. Of course it would be to Lesley's advantage too to try to get Pritch to act as go-between for Joyce and me, and in turn, to see how the wind blew as far as she and I were concerned. One big harmonious family. I wondered where they would decide to send me to college, since that was to their minds probably the ideal place for me to go. Or would they, this Board of Directors, make some other plans—all depending on whether I was going to make a happy addition to the family or not? I decided to take up the die—and cast it straight in his face.

"I'm not overly fond of Lesley either," I told him with emphasis, but no particular feeling.

"I didn't ask you that," he said slowly, but interrupting me all the same. "What I really want to know is if you are going to be happy in New York."

"I doubt it!" I cried impatiently. "But I didn't come back here to be happy. I've got other plans."

"Such as?" He looked at me measuringly.

"Skip it," I said. "I won't interfere with your lives—the Bradford-Allyns and the Bradford-Longtrees."

"I understand how you feel," he looked at me with a sort of odious fraternal protectiveness, "but there's no use in jumping to conclusions."

I was so mad I almost jumped out of the cab. "Look here, Pritchard Allyn, if you think I want to gain a brother you're mistaken! Anyway, you're sounding more like Mother Hen. When I tell you I want no part of any of you, I mean it! I intend to live in New York for a short time—maybe with Avery or somebody, move into my own flat—then leave. I hate being around all of you. I think it was simply awful of you and Lesley to turn up at the airport, beaming like a pair of relatives. I want no part of you, her, or your marriage."

"Are you really that jealous of Lesley?"

"What did you expect?" I almost shouted.

"I thought when you saw us at the airport that you would—"

"—Throw my arms around your necks as you did around mine and crow like a baby fed on Pet Milk? The next thing you'll be telling me is that like a good bridegroom you've confessed all, that Lesley wept and forgave, and to prove how courageous and understanding she is, she wants me for her best friend *and* her maid of honor. Stop the taxi, or I will. I'm getting out." I was shaking like a vibrating machine, and the driver had slowed down and was surveying the situation over his shoulder.

Pritch grabbed my arm and firmly drew me back. "Now listen," he said sternly, angrily. "Keep it under wraps. Here, driver. We'll get out here."

"We certainly will!" I said and jerked open the door and tried to slam it in Pritch's face.

He skillfully fixed that, and grabbed me again too, and propelled me across Fifth Avenue into Ninth Street. "Steady," he warned. "Or I'll break off your arm and stuff it down your throat."

What is the answer to this? Certainly, he had me in his grasp, as the saying goes, and I could feel the tips of his fingers boring in. There would be some pretty black and blue marks left, if he ever took his fingers off, that is.

We entered a walk-up, or rather a walk-down, and he pushed me straight ahead toward a white door. No fumbling for the key. He opened it with the swift skill of a house-breaker. He sort of flung me aside, once we were in, and walked over to a closet where obviously he kept the liquor. But I was wrong. He had gone to get a sweater instead, and was shedding his tie, vest and jacket in order to put it on. What a nerve he had, thinking that he felt a little cold at a time like this!

Now I saw that the apartment was one extra-long, and wide room, furnished in beautiful early American antiques, and that the liquor was kept on a dry sink on one side of the room toward which Pritch now strode.

He held up the Scotch bottle in brisk question toward me. I stormily turned my head and he poured two walloping whale-sized drinks, rattled some ice from an ice bucket, and added water from a pitcher. "Now," he said. "Sit down before you really make me mad."

Cool, taking my time, raising my eyebrows in answer to his look, I sat down on the antique settee across the room from him.

"You really are a wild one, aren't you?" he asked.

"When I have ample reasons for making me wild," I replied.

"You nearly made me wild too. I almost never lose my temper."

"Oh, Pritch," I said forlornly. "Look. Don't let's go on with this. You've said enough. I've said enough. I can't help how I feel. Maybe it's wild, or willful—or selfish, or whatever. But I *am* upset."

"And so am I." His voice was quiet, regretful.

"I know you think you've hurt me, well, you have, but…"

"I've hurt Lesley more," he cut in, in the same quiet voice.

"Why? She'll get over it. Just because you told her about our little reunion in London. How could that mean anything to her?"

"It doesn't to her. It does to me. I think. At least that's why we've called the whole thing off. I was going to write you—only I couldn't think how to put it. Then Bart and Joycie told us you were coming back—"

I looked at the half of the drink I had spilled in my lap. Cautiously, my hand still like the last stages of palsy, I eased the glass over to a table. Easy, girl. Easy! was the only idiotic thing I found I had to say to myself. Certainly, the real thinking part of me had just been short circuited. With a loud explosion. I could still feel the reverberation of it in every nerve. "Do Joyce and Bart know that—that you and Lesley—?"

"Have called it off?" He finished for me. "Joyce does. But Lesley and Joyce want you to tell Bart. When you decide…" his face was deeply troubled and pale, as if he had just cried a lot. His eyes were pleading.

"When I decide what?" I heard my voice saying from a great distance.

"When you decide whether or not you'd like to marry me."

Chapter Seven

"Well, aren't you the sly-boots scandal-maker!" Avery greeted me when I went to the phone, and before I could make reply, she continued, "Everybody in town knows that Lesley broke her engagement after you and Pritch had a little night on the town in London."

"What?" I said lamely, but I felt lame. Lame, but serene.

"Am I *persona non* at your address?" she went on. "I'd like to see you. I won't even ask for inside stories, even though I'm sort of ghosting a gossip column these days."

I asked her which one, and when she named it I immediately decided she was lying; that she was just hoping for the job. "When do you start?" I needled her.

"This minute unless you display the proper attitude. What I don't know about you, *Mother!*"

That word still made me a little sensitive, even though things were all set: Pritch and I were flying down to Florida next week. Florida was his mother's idea—don't ask me why. Probably because it was still off-season and "reasonable," as well as remote. Anything to humor the in-laws. Besides, I am sentimental, and what could be nicer than letting the bride pick her own orange blossoms? But this news was not for

Avery's ears, columnist or not. The fact that Pritch and I were to be married was very hush-hush. We'd simply turn up in that blissful state a few weeks from now.

I laughed at Avery fondly and invited her to meet me for drinks at the Plaza.

"After five," she said.

Maybe she really was working.

We agreed on the time and hung up.

Joycie asked me who had called. I told her, and in such a way that she would know I considered it none of her business.

She made her usual anti-Avery face. "Pritch agrees with us about her, you know."

"Oh, bug off," I said under my breath and walked upstairs to the nursery—which I forcibly shared with my fretful and very spoiled nephew as a bedroom, since the only other bedroom besides theirs was for the nurse who "slept in." Joyce was being very heroic, thrifty and housewifely these days. She had only a cleaning woman who came in twice a week, in addition to the nurse. The rest of the time she took care of everything herself—including the cooking; and I'll staunchly say she certainly took care of that. Poor Bart. I wondered if even Joyce truly liked tapioca. Anyway, there must have been some better way to make it. The whole thing—this crazy economy drive, the sloppy housekeeping, the bad cooking—made me sick. When I thought of the perfect order the house used to have, the rich, magnificent dinners Tennie served, all those guests, Mother… But it was not my affair.

At any rate, miraculously, somehow, I was getting everything I wanted. Absolutely everything. With Pritch, and the very definite prospect of a little Pritch, the Beautiful People were back in full flower. And I had made up my mind too that as soon as Pritch and I were actually married and settled down in a comfortable house or large apartment, I would ask Tennie and Jess back to work for us. No cramped quarters for the Pritchard Allyn IIIs!

Of course it would mean using my money, since Pritch in his own right had only an allowance, but who could object to good property as an investment? Besides, Joyce and Bart—or at least Joyce—were dying to unload their share of the Glen Cove house, boarded up now since Mother's death, and going to pot—and maybe Pritch and I could buy them out. Or else I could sell too. In any case, there were countless solutions, and I was as busy with ideas as a portable IBM machine.

The afternoon simply took off, and I right after it. Time was comet-fast to me these days; there was so much to do, to see about, think about. And then there was love. Love, a warm, luxurious blanket over everything, shutting out the awful, the cold, the noise. Every day there was Pritch.

I called him to say I was seeing Avery; despite what Joyce thought, I knew Pritch trusted me to trust my own judgment in such matters. And I was delighted to report to Joyce that not only had Pritch made no objection, but had even suggested that I bring Avery along to Ninth Street to join us for dinner. I told her with such bitchy pleasure, that she reacted with the affronted alarm of a mother insulted by a small child.

Just to further enhance the effect I asked her if she really wanted me to stick my tongue out at her.

"You forget this is my house," she said, her nose wings dilated.

"Oh, go back to your comic book!" I advised her, making a home hit. Joyce had simply loved comic books in our childhood.

"I'll be glad when you're gone!" this inspired her to say.

"How gracious of you to tell me," I replied, but I was surprised and hurt by the vehemence of her dislike.

"I don't care! You should see yourself. You're bad, bad—all the way through. Far worse even than your mother!"

"Whose house did you say this was?" I asked icily.

"I don't care! Bart is my husband and it's going to stay that way. I'm no Lesley, uh-uh! You can't snatch away from me what belongs to me!"

"Are you suggesting Bart is next on my list?" I asked in scornful amusement.

"You're not above incest, if that's what you mean!"

I looked at her coldly, levelly. Her still-pretty, but tired face was distorted with anger. And her hair was all awful today. Also she was wearing a perfect bag of a dress and a pair of runover shoes. "You are a terrible mess, Joycie," I said. "Inside and out."

"At least I'm not what you are!"

"You can say that again, fishwife," I told her and went out of the house, slamming the door.

How do you like that? I kept saying over and over to myself. I almost called Bart. But things were bad enough with them—obviously. And my own threshold of pain was still low. Better let the whole thing ride. I'd soon be riding out, and forever, with my Beautiful People.

While I was trying to get a cab, it started to rain, and I made up my mind then and there that the first thing Pritch and I would buy would be a car. Pity I hadn't bought one on the other side.

And while I was riding along, my conscious mind, stuck and pivoted on deep subjects like that: how I needed a car, how hard it was to get taxis in the rain, how Avery would probably not be on time since she never was, etc. But underneath I was as upset as hell. The quarrel with Joycie had really shaken me. In the first place it was bad and rocky to absolutely *know* our rift was permanent, and that Bart, so long as they were married, would have to stay on her side. Which made me feel scary. What if something went wrong with me and Pritch? I'd be even more alone than I had been before. And the baby thing: I still hadn't told him I thought I was pregnant. At first—a few days ago—it had seemed such a warm and lovely idea that I thought I would save it, as a sort of wedding present. Then I realized I was kidding myself about it: the truth was I was scared to tell him. He might not want it; it might change him—and everything. I wanted terribly to talk to someone about it, and semi-consciously knew Avery had been elected. But I would be insane—as well as disloyal to Pritch—to tell her now. Was she trustworthy? Did she have all the good sense I remembered her having? Maybe, I thought, I should just find a good abortionist. But that thought nearly killed me.

Anyway, when I walked into the Plaza she was right there, looking as bright and beautiful as ever, and told me at once that I looked awful.

"I see we're taking up where we left off," I said, feeling miserable but cheered a little—no, comforted is a better word—at the sight of her. "I see you've cut your hair."

"Yes," she said, touching her almost white-blonde curls. "I'm far too sophisticated these days to wear it child-style—long. See yours is still long," she twinkled at me mischievously, giving my own coif a good look.

"Okay. Say it."

"Looks divine," she answered. "Going to cut it for the wedding?"

"Whose?" I inquired with young-cat innocence. "Lesley's and Pritch's?"

"Get you!" she cried in amusement. "Trying to enter diplomatic service? Or are you brainwashing me? Wait 'til you see tomorrow's paper."

"Okay," I gave up. "I'll tell you all about it and you kill the story. Or I'll kill you."

"Why so secretive? Everybody knows it. Far better to be above-board than below."

"Maybe," I said thoughtfully. "But I hate all this mess, believe it or not."

"I believe you, Clo," she told me with quiet sincerity.

It was good, awfully good to have a friend.

We went into the Oak Room and had a couple of martinis. Then I asked her to go down with me to Pritch's and join us for dinner. She was almost touchingly pleased by the invitation and accepted at once.

"I'm sort of on the loose these days, you know," she told me. "You know Madre died."

"No," I said in genuine surprise. "I *am* sorry, Avery."

"Yes," she went on. "And now I know how you felt when—when your mother died. You see, Madre wasn't like just any old grandmother—"

She gave me the details, and went on to say that the Southampton house had been sold for practically nothing. "Of course I have a little money now. But I hate it, really. I so much preferred having Madre."

"I know," I said, because I did. I felt closer to Avery in that moment than I'd ever felt to any friend I'd ever had, including Joyce. Maybe that's what made me suddenly decide to tell her about the baby.

I could tell she was rather horrified. Not at my conduct, but at my predicament. "You've *got* to tell Pritch," she said at once. "Don't wait another minute."

"Why?" I asked.

"Because if you don't," she said, then paused. "Look here, do you know his family well?"

I told her I didn't; in fact not at all. I'd simply met them the evening Pritch and I had made up our minds. "They seemed rather nice—"

"They're cruddy," she said flatly. "About as broadminded as Savonorola. And as vindictive."

I had to admit I didn't remember Savonorola too well.

She sighed, looking distressed. "Well, look here," she explained. "They're heap-big church pillars, number one—where do you think Pritch got all his religious mania from?"

"Aren't they Episcopalians—I mean, sort of high?" I asked.

"Sure, but who says because you're high church you have to be casual about it?"

I pondered this, and at length voiced aloud the theory that I thought they would have objected on the spot, the night they met me, if they were going to object at all.

"I don't mean that," Avery said brushing this notion aside. "You probably think yourself much worse than they do."

"But wouldn't they remember that I was engaged before and broke it up and all?"

"Probably not, even if the word had reached their remote ears. Nobody keeps scrapbooks about us, you know. Besides, they are the kind of conservative squares who have no interest in gossip columns or anything like that."

"Well, that's something, anyway," I said in relief.

"But this baby thing is something else," she said, still sounding disturbed. "They'll think Pritch broke up with Lesley to make an honest woman of you—or that you've tricked him into marrying you and giving your baby his name."

"They wouldn't!" I protested.

"They might," she assured me. "In any case, this is something you *must* discuss with Pritch. After all, it's as much his business as it is yours!"

She was right, of course.

Chapter Eight

When I told Pritch I was pregnant he turned the color of a glass of milk. "My God, Chloe!" he exclaimed and just stared at me.

I guess I looked pretty miserable, because he came over and put his arms around me and said, "Don't cry, sweetheart. I think it's great about the kid. But you're so damned young, and…are you absolutely sure?"

"Pretty sure," I said, looking up at him, not at all certain that he did find it so great.

"Well, God, this *is* something," he murmured, as if he were thinking out loud.

I didn't say anything; it wasn't up to me. I had told him, and that was that.

"What would you have done," he asked, "if this thing with Lesley hadn't—"

"If you and Lesley had gone ahead with your plans? I would have gone on with mine." Then I told him how I had come back here specifically to see Avery and arrange for an abortion, or to have the baby, depending on what seemed best.

"You poor kid," he said sadly, shaking his head over and

over. He sat down beside me and took my hand in his and sort of laced our fingers together. "I feel very deeply about these things, Chloe—marriage, babies," he told me quietly, earnestly, his head close to mine. "I would never have forgiven myself."

"You wouldn't have known," I said gently.

This made him shake his head all the more, and his face had the drawn yet relieved look of a man who has narrowly escaped a fatal accident. Finally he more or less came out of it. "Well," he said. "Well." Then he smiled at me, his face brightening like a clearing day. "I guess a celebration is in order. Where the hell is Avery? It doesn't take an hour to buy a package of butts."

"She probably got waylaid," I said, cheering too.

He gave me a sharp look. "You can say that again. I suppose you told her?"

I nodded. "But she's the only one."

Pritch and I were sitting in his apartment, and now that we had had our talk I felt super-giddy and restless. "God, darling, those draperies are *filthy*!" I exclaimed. "Are they washable? Let's take them down and wash them."

He found this perfectly ludicrous. "In the first place, Chloe Longtree, you never washed anything in your life except yourself. And in the second place you can't wash things like that. They have to be cleaned. What kind of wife am I getting anyway? Even Lesley has better sense than that."

I swatted him one, which he more or less eluded, and told him to shut his cotton-picking mouth about old has-beens.

"Anyway, let's take them down," I said. "Don't we want everything clean and bridal when we get back from Florida?"

He sort of nodded his head, then looked vaguely preoccupied. I asked him what it was.

"Nothing. Only I more or less promised the elders we'd stay uptown with them after we come back—until we find a place of our own."

"What's wrong with this?" I protested immediately. "I love this place!"

"Oh, Chloe, honey, it's not nearly big enough for two people, and I'd planned all along to give it up. My lease expires at the end of the month." I guess I looked disappointed, because he said, "Baby doll. It'll work out. We'll find something we like. It won't take long."

I was all for looking now, for the thought of staying with the senior Allyns in that huge old apartment of theirs had suddenly become like a combination of going back to Aunt Maude's mausoleum and Juliet's tomb. But I kept this to myself. "It doesn't matter," I shrugged it off. "Anyway, we haven't gone yet, and we can always stay in a hotel when we get back if we haven't found something."

He gave me a strange kind of look, but pursued the subject no further. All the same, I felt as if we had had our first husband-wife tiff. And I wondered if he had the most minute inkling of how little I liked the idea of joining the Allyn parents. Marriage, as a friend of mine once said, certainly makes strange bedfellows.

Avery, who had deliberately found a pretext for going out so I could speak to Pritch in private, was indeed greatly overdue.

Pritch began to pace around the flat, getting more and more like a restless hyena, because he was awfully hungry. And upset, was my addenda to his complaint—the former also unvoiced. I was going to be a tactful wife if it killed me.

"And it probably will," Avery told me while we were in the ladies' room of the restaurant, whence we had repaired so I could tell her how everything went. "Pritch is very difficult. And stubborn." She gave herself a good run-down in the looking-glass, checking to see that all seams were straight, all hairs perfect. Then we went back to join Pritch.

We were having dinner at Henri Soule's "cheap" place which had just opened across from the St. Regis. Only Pritch took on like the bill had given him an ulcer when he saw the amount. I was quite embarrassed, and would have suggested taking care of it myself. Except, as I say, I was going to be a tactful wife.

"From now on," Pritch said outside in the street, "we eat TV dinners."

"Or crow," I heard Avery whisper under her breath, her expression violently disapproving of the scene he was still making.

"You may be rich, Chloe, but I emphatically am not," he addressed me again angrily.

I felt this was no time to discuss finances, and suggested we get a cab back to his place. But I could see from his slightly scowling expression that he really wanted to be alone.

He took a look at his watch. "Aw, Christ!" he said in exasperation, giving both Avery and me rude looks to match his voice.

I said nothing, but Avery spoke up: "Were you going somewhere?" she inquired.

"I was going to study," he said unpleasantly. "If I'd known having dinner would have taken all this time I would have suggested we eat in the Village."

"I'm sorry, darling," I said smoothly, feeling this was the time to step in. I knew his present griping was really left over from his annoyance at the size of the dinner check. It really had upset him, and I wondered why: I happened to know he had at the moment quite a lot of money with him. And this invention about having to study…had it been a fact, he would have mentioned it earlier. Was he trying to get rid of us, or what? "I think I'll go home," I said tentatively.

"Oh, sweetie, don't do that!" he said instantly. "I don't really have to study very long, and anyway the book I need I haven't got—this character in my class, who apparently owns no books at all, but borrows everybody else's, still has it."

"Why don't you get it back from him?" I asked, feeling very confused by his off-again on-again behavior. "Where does he live?"

"He lives in the Village."

"Well, why can't we simply stop by there on the way to your house and you go in and pick it up?"

"I'd rather not," Pritch said uncomfortably.

Avery gave me a secret look and formed the word "diffi-cult" with her lips. I could see what she meant. But every-thing couldn't be hearts-and-flowers perfect; he had to have some bad traits. Even nasty ones. I wanted a human being, didn't I?

I doubt if Pritch saw Avery make her unspoken comment, but he did notice that I was silent and musing, because he hastily started to offer up his reason for not wanting to pay the call, however circumlocutious the way. "I guess I ought to go by there," he said, "because this fellow has a couple of other books of mine too."

"Well, why don't you then?" Avery wanted to know. "Don't you like the guy? I wouldn't let him con *me* into letting him borrow my books if I didn't like him—"

"Oh, I like him all right. In fact, he's sort of a funny character—one of the true-blue children of the Beat Generation. West Coast displaced poet cum philosopher cum jazz aficionado—primitive jazz, of course—going to Columbia on thin air, as far as I can see, though he must have at least a scholarship."

"What's his name?" Avery said, her eyes oddly bright.

"Seymour—I forget his last name."

"Well how are you going to ring the bell of his apartment if you don't know his last name?"

"His apartment? Good God, I guess you *would* have to call it an apartment. But it certainly doesn't have a bell. It's up about eighty-five flights of the most dangerous stairs you've ever walked on, and when you get there it's a sort of loft—and more or less furnished like one."

"Sounds fright-making," Avery said, and I agreed.

"Anyway," Pritch said rather slyly, "I've forgotten which street it's on."

"You devil!" Avery cried. "Tantalizing us like this! How

do you know I wouldn't like to meet some beat type and have a nice untidy love affair with him? I've never had a man in blue jeans and a beard—the Bohemian works."

"If you met this one he wouldn't stay in blue jeans long—not from what he tells me, at any rate. He says he likes 'society dolls,' makes him really feel like East meets West—"

"Or West meets East—" Avery giggled. "He sounds divine. I've got to have him for my very own."

"Well, he grows on you," Pritch admitted.

"There," I said, "you have the full definition of a parasite." They both missed it. Avery through absorption, and Pritch for some reason. But I hoped Avery wouldn't get too worked up over the notion of this Seymour. I had already decided he was nothing I needed to meet, no matter how she felt, and I could now understand Pritch's reluctance to visit him. Pritch is very fastidious—to the point of making me look like "Craig's Husband"—and I knew if this book borrower's premises were not clean, it would make Pritch miserable to have to put a foot in the door. I doubted even if Pritch had any intention really of ever trying to get the books back; he probably did not want them after they had been nesting in such repellent-sounding quarters.

All the way to the Village, Avery kept teasing Pritch to have the driver take us over in the direction where Pritch thought this peculiar one lived.

Pritch, however, shook his head firmly; as Avery had said, he was stubborn. "No, we're going to my place and have a nice drink. Wouldn't you like that better?"

"Better than what?" Avery sulked.

"Better than smoking marijuana, for instance," Pritch told her. "Which is the only refreshment he'd offer you."

"How exciting!" Avery exclaimed. "I've never had any. Really, now, Pritch," she pleaded, "can't we go? Just for a few minutes?"

"No," he said staunchly. "Neither of you is dressed for it."

"You make it sound like a hunting trip," Avery pouted, her eyes large and reproachful.

I knew he meant it, and I also knew now that the real reason he didn't want to go was not the distasteful disorder probably to be found, but because he simply did not want to get mixed up too closely with people like that. It was all very well to be hail-fellow-well-met on campus, and even lend books (and possibly money), but no *confrère* business.

By this time we had reached Pritch's apartment, and the cab stopped, and Pritch helped me out. Then Avery. She lagged a little, her heart still set, it was quite evident, on meeting this denizen of the Village. She had no need for disappointment, for there on the stoop, obviously waiting for someone, was a young man who couldn't possibly be anyone but the Seymour in question.

Chapter Nine

"Hiya, dad," the person signaled Pritch casually, and without being asked, simply followed us inside the door, even while Pritch was still in the "why, hello there" process. I noticed our caller had a couple of books under his arm.

Once inside, and introduced, Seymour nodded to us, and said nothing, as if he hadn't bothered to listen to our names. However, this didn't mean he found us of no interest. When I say he "sized us up" I kid you not. He measured every inch of us, beginning, of course, with breasts, legs, and buttocks. Then we got it in the face. Then our clothes. I started to remark that I was not auditioning for a spot in the chorus line, when he simply turned away and ignored us the rest of the time he was there. He talked exclusively to Pritch, and it was like listening to a dictionary of Beatnik argot. He kept using words like "cool" which was about the only one I recognized, though he made it clear after he switched off campus talk and on to his vivid private life that "going steady with Mary Jane" and "turning on" meant smoking marijuana—or "pot," as he continually called it.

Pritch looked embarrassed and disgusted, and was only too glad when Seymour hauled his obviously sockless sneaker-clad feet to the floor and looked as if he were standing up to go. Instead, he said, "Mind if I have a private *mot* with you, man?"

"Not at all," Pritch said stiffly, and they retreated to the hallway, almost out of my line of vision. But not too far out; after a few seconds of animated but whispered talk on Seymour's part, I saw Pritch nervously shake his head, then reach in his pocket for his wallet. I looked at Avery, but she couldn't see from where she sat, so I decided it was better to just say nothing.

"He thinks we're squares," Avery remarked with feeling.

"He doesn't think we are—I mean, that we exist."

"He doesn't think, period," Avery went further. "If he's a Beat boy, they must have their definition wrong, or else their grammar—he's not beat, he's destroyed."

Then Pritch and Beat Boy came back, both looking somewhat shaken; Pritch for lending money, Seymour for borrowing it. Both knew that the transaction was closed forever, from the looks on their faces. You did not need to study Seymour's visage and attire too hard to know that anything he termed "borrowed" to him meant "gift." His returning the books was an act of barter.

"Now that you've brought back this thing," Pritch indicated one of the books Seymour had given him, "I guess I really will have to study."

"You mean you're throwing us out?" Avery said, looking rather more crestfallen than I had expected. How could she be enjoying this?

"Why don't we all go out and have a coffee first?" asked

Seymour quite intelligibly.

"All right," Pritch gave in. "I suppose it can wait."

I shot Avery a thorough look as the four of us started out. I couldn't tell whether she was fascinated or bored, attracted or repelled. She was a strange one sometimes. But judging by the avidity with which she had accepted our dinner invitation tonight, I guessed she was very lonely. And I could guess why too. It had started a long time ago, while we were both going to Chalmers—or maybe even before that, because of her mother. Avery, and her mother before her, had been as thriftless with her friends and reputation as though they were money; the always-plenty-more-where-that-came-from routine. I never did know why, because she was as good-looking as hell and could have had anybody if she'd cared to be selective. But she wasn't, and she had been in the habit of dropping anyone who suggested she improve her ways. I never did, nor, of course, did the Yalies who used to be so crazy about her. But now, I gathered, when the Yale boys called it was more apt to be at dawn's early light, rather than in the gloaming, when proper dates are made with proper people. Now, poor thing, she seemed to reaping all the chaff and none of the grain from that improvident sowing. But I hoped she wouldn't settle for Seymour—that was too far out.

Why didn't I like him? Well, in the first place people in peculiar clothes make me uncomfortable, but the real reason was, and I admit it, that he ignored me. Or rather he looked at me as if I were a commercial product, however a superior one, labeled "doll" with "rich and pretty" in parentheses beside it And I can't stand to be depersonalized. Admittedly, had he exuded charm, been attentive, I would have reacted quite differently, for he was quite good-looking and so was the beard, and his eyes were very expressive, and in a way quite lovely.

And, as it turned out, Avery had the same reaction. It seems he kept calling her—abstractly speaking, of course, and carefully employing the third person—"a rich square dame," insensitive and uncaring for "life." She was really quite furious, and after reporting these results of their chat as they walked along together, she practically turned on Pritch, as if it were all his fault. "Is *that* all you have to offer?" she asked him several times, precisely as if Pritch had deliberately arranged the whole thing, to sell her to the Beat Generation, with Seymour acting as representative.

Pritch kept excusing him, saying it was one of Seymour's off nights, that he was really shy—that was the trouble—and finally adding that he had seemed quite high on pot, and didn't we think so.

"I thought he was high on wine of self," Avery said very heatedly.

Maybe if she hadn't been yakking so much, or if I hadn't become involved to the extent where I was trying to keep her from pulverizing Pritch and Pritch from becoming really quite annoyed, it would never have happened. I was telling them to shut up being angry about one angry young man or whatever it was, and just about that time was when the Corvette skidded up on the curb at Sheridan Square where we were waiting for the eternal taxi, and I got knocked down.

I got right up again, full of Village grime and mud-puddle samples but fine otherwise. Not even any torn nylons or bruises. I assured the driver to this effect who said the accident was due to a mechanical failure of some kind, and that he'd been en route to his garage when he got me instead. We exchanged names and telephone numbers just in case, and he took off while we shakily climbed into a cab.

Nobody said it, but everybody thought it: would this have any unfortunate result on my state of motherhood?

I guess I'll never know for sure, but it certainly was eminently apparent two days after we were married that if I ever had been pregnant, I was no longer. It made me extremely sad, actually, and it made Pritch pensive at least.

"I suppose I never should have told Mother and Dad," he mused.

"You told *them*?" I asked, so horrified that I could not keep from showing it.

"Yes," he said coolly. "Anything wrong in that?"

I shook my head, knowing anything else was folly. I couldn't even quote Dr. Johnson's: "I have furnished you with an explanation; I cannot furnish you with an understanding," for I wasn't even prepared to go along with the explanation bit. All I had was a feeling that their knowing boded the most negative of no good.

Chapter Ten

Naturally, our honeymoon was something of a frost. We made all the motions and ostensibly had a gay old time. We stayed in a terribly wonderful place in Sarasota and met a lot of people who were fun. But somehow, even the wedding itself was sort of anti-climactic, and I kept getting the awful feeling that Pritch was brooding about Lesley, especially after the baby thing.

Being the wifely diplomat, I didn't come right out and ask to explore his guilt feelings with him, but I did suggest we go back to New York before we'd planned; things were that rocky.

He neither agreed nor protested; we simply took a plane. I had found out these past few weeks that this husband of mine was a silent partner. He hardly said anything all the way to New York, all of which made me as delirious with joy as a throbbing tooth. What can he be thinking? I kept thinking. And it always came back to the same thing: he thinks he's made a mistake, that he should have married Lesley instead. And I reached the point where I halfway agreed with him. But I was determined to make this marriage work—all the way. I did love him very much, even sore and silent as he was.

I hadn't forgotten he could laugh and be a warm and lovely Pritch, even if he had.

Consequently, when we left the air terminal and got into a cab, the question of our destination wasn't even discussed: he simply gave his parents' address.

As we rode along that night on those traffic-jammed streets, the city reminded me of my own mental insides—hysterical noise, too much going on at once, no order, and everything panicky with outrage and paranoia. Seemingly insoluble. Yet the streets cleared every night, albeit late at night, and so would I. But wouldn't it be too late? I longed to talk it over with someone. If only my brother Bart were not so all fenced in by his marriage and the family bit. He would help. Maybe he would anyway. Maybe I could meet him for a lunch or a drink tomorrow, away from Joyce. At that moment, it didn't occur to me to appeal to good old Avery.

"Here we are," Pritch stirred me from my thinking, and indeed, there we were—just outside the great, dark old structure where his parents lived, and where I would live too, for a time—or die.

The driver and Pritch unloaded us, while I stood shivering on the sidewalk, bunched up in my Florida-weight coat. Then we went inside.

Even the elevator had that warm mahogany gleam that all handsome old buildings have, and momentarily I felt quiet and reassured. This respite lasted even while Pritch nervously rang the bell, then fiddled for the key. He was just about to use it when an ancient shuffled to the door, opened it, her face an Actor's Studio classic of suspicion, and said, "Oh,"—

nothing more as she stood aside to let us pass.

"Hello Olga," he said pleasantly, just as if she had expressed overjoyment at seeing us. "Where is everybody?"

"Out," she said sternly, as if this were an eviction notice instead of an answer to his question.

He made no comment; there was none to make since he had telephoned them the night before, and they knew we were due back. He didn't even turn to me and say, that's strange.

"Maybe, darling," said I, "they thought we weren't coming directly here." Certainly, I hadn't in spite of his earlier suggestion that this was what we would do. Somehow, down in Florida, I had thought he'd come around to my way of thinking, and had more or less decided that we should go to the Pierre or the Plaza or something until we established ourselves. But when people don't talk much, you never know.

In any event, Pritch didn't answer. Instead he said, and not to me but the ancient, "I guess they'll be back soon," and instructed her to "put Mrs. Allyn's things in the guest room."

From the look she gave him, I thought she was going to ask him to put them there himself. Then she gave me a very thorough visual going-over and left without a word.

I hadn't missed the guest-room thing, but at the moment it didn't carry any particular significance for me. I was too puzzled by Olga. "Is she a woodwork product, or just what?" I asked.

"She loves my mother and hates me," Pritch said, strolling about the living room, whence I had followed him, fingering this and that "See?" he said. "Isn't this place awful?"

I wanted to remind him that I had seen it once before, however briefly, and that he had fully prepared me for it that night in London when he had compared it so unfavorably to Aunt Maude's splendor.

"It's not bad, darling," I said, and then with my new-found spouse diplomacy subtly inserted: "we don't *have* to stay here, you know. I'm sure it's an imposition."

"They want it that way," he said, accenting the "they," as if they were foreign agents who had us in their power.

"Well, show me around then," I said brightly. "I want to know where everything is if I'm to live here."

"You'll have your own room," he told me flatly, as if we had been having a long argument about it.

And that's when I simply collapsed on that hideous gray cat-colored overstuffed couch and cried and cried and cried. It was no wifely wile to bring him around; I meant it. But he responded as smoothly as if I'd done it on purpose.

"Chloe, Chloe, Chloe," he murmured over and over, stroking my hair. Then he put his arms around me, and kissed me until I stopped sobbing; then we got up and he led me to his bedroom.

It was wonderful and we were truly together again, only have you ever had your brand new in-laws walk in and find you making love? That's what happened. They ducked right out again, looking after a flash of horrified surprise as if they had merely opened the wrong closet door. Pritch somehow summoned the stamina to give a false chuckle over it. "They'll get used to it," he said.

"Then why am I in the guest room if they approve of

legal lovemaking?" I asked as I hurried into my clothes.

"Mother thought it would be best for your health," Pritch replied; meaning, of course, my pregnant health.

I thought a million divine things to say to that, but censored them all myself. "Do you really think," I asked instead, "that it wouldn't be wiser now to wait until morning to go out and say hello? If we don't, maybe they'll just think we're tired from the trip."

But I sensed his negative answer, even before it came, and went on with my dressing. I looked about his room and thought how depressing to have grown up here, and wondered if the guest room were any better. Probably the lumber room, I decided, judging by the rest of the house.

So far, I had seen little of it, but that was too much. The place *was* big, and if the furnishings lacked style, the architecture did not. All of which made the elder Allyn's acquisitions somehow worse. Everything was like the couch—comfortable, but stiff in feeling, humdrum and unfriendly. This house had real Presbyterian austerity, to quote a phrase I read somewhere. I doubted very much then that the Allyns would have even consented to something so frivolous as a listing in the *Social Register*, presuming that they were up to it, society- and family-wise. A large assumption. Well…here I was. We made our smiling appearance, hand in hand.

Mr. Allyn, who looked a great deal like Pritch, took my hand in a firm howdy-do type shake, and Mrs. Allyn pecked at my cheek—literally—and said, "Call me 'Mother,' dear." I was glad when she took her hands off my shoulders.

Then we all sat down and beamed at each other, and all

became uncomfortably aware that Olga was hovering in the velvet hung doorway which separated the living room from the next.

"Come in, Olga," Mrs. Allyn called in false brightness, touching a hand to her cat-colored gray hair which exactly matched her couch.

And in Olga came. "She's almost deaf," my mother-in-law explained to me in a very theatrical aside. Then she said to the servant, "Come in, dear, come in!" And I got my formal introduction to Olga, and was pronounced a member of the family. She took this with her former good grace, gave me a good glare, and switched haltingly to her other foot.

Mother Allyn made some servant-mistress talk about luggage, if there were enough eggs for breakfast, and similar things which sounded so studiedly rehearsed to make me feel at home that I felt positively lost in a forest. And sunk.

Then Father Allyn inquired about our trip, and Pritch told him at such length about our sightseeing, our trip through the Ringling Museum, the circus people, etc., that I could see the poor man's eyes glaze with boredom. All the while, I knew, Mrs. Allyn was boning up on me. She had evaluated my clothes, analyzed my skin, had me down for a nervous type, and was probably planning to tell me what to do with my hair, when Pritch made an elaborate yawn and said we were tired and had better go to bed.

"That's right, Brother," she said to him, utterly serious— that's what she called him; and, looking at me solicitously added, "our new little daughter has to take very good care of herself."

Oh, my God, I thought as Pritch and I exchanged kisses (after the parents turn, of course) and parted for the night; and not so much as a nightcap. Here, I knew already, that term strictly applied to an antiquated, but sensible, form of headdress.

Chapter Eleven

I won't say that living in the Allyn household was a new life for me, but it was, if deadly, not without its moments, and certainly it was different. And in a way, refreshing.

Pritch and I were summoned from our separate rooms at eight to come to the breakfast table that first morning. And Mother Allyn was as cheery and as active as a robin. She made it quite clear in every way that she liked her life, loved her husband and son, and didn't care a damn (if she had been able to bring herself to utter that word) whether I was Chloe Longtree or Chloe by the song of the same name. I was to her simply her son's wife, and she wanted with all of her wholesome heart to accept me. And I admired her tremendously.

I had known lots of middle-class people before, of the "well-to-do" but modest circumstances group, but I had never been very close to them. Living at the Allyns was therefore a real thing for me. Their rigid sense of morality was completely alien, slightly appalling, but their rigid sense of justice was not. I suppose all might have gone well had the two in our case not been so inextricably mixed together.

It began with my money. Mother Allyn and I were having

one of our quiet mother-daughter talks one morning after the "men" had gone to school and office respectively, when I told her we were looking for a house to buy. "House?" said Mother Allyn. "Why, dear, that doesn't seem a bit wise."

"Why?" I asked—innocently, I realized now, so at-home had I become. "Real estate is an awfully good investment. Pritch agrees with me, I know. It's crazy not to in the circumstances—" ("Circumstances," of course was a euphemistic reference to our expected child, which we had decided not to tell the parents was no longer expected.)

"Well," she said, settling back against her chair, looking thoughtful, "it would be *nice* to buy a house, but Father gives Brother all he can afford just now—he plans to retire soon, you know—and until Brother—Pritch—finishes his education…well, I don't see how financially—"

That's when I realized that Mother and Father Allyn knew nothing at all about me. "I could swing it," I said quietly.

The look that came over her face would do justice to a Dr. Jekyll-Mr. Hyde performance. At the end she was literally speechless.

"I have lots of money, Mother Allyn," I said, and proceeded to tell her about it.

I can't say for sure, but I think that is when the real hostility started. "Of course," she said, after I'd finished, "that does make a great deal of difference. I didn't realize that Brother—Pritch, as you call him—had married an heiress." She almost added a "huummph." "I recall that he said you had a private income"—she gestured, as if she had just laid it aside and put me on the balance scale instead—"but I hadn't realized that—well, in that case, you certainly don't need *my* financial counsel."

"I do indeed," I told her. "I haven't anybody else's—except my lawyer's and broker's."

"I'm afraid I'm not up to either," she said, standing up. "I just hope you'll use your money judiciously, and not let it spoil—you." I knew her hesitation over that last word was caused by an indecision as to whether she should say "spoil Pritch"—or "Brother," to put it her style—or me.

"Well," she said in an airy tone which told me she was on the verge of making some excuse for closing the audience, "I expect you have lots to do today." (She thought I was going to shop for maternity clothes.) She turned and gave me a great rigid smile that was supposed to be a beam, but her eyes were as hard and cold as rocks.

"Yes, I have lots to do," I murmured. "I'm lunching with my brother, for one thing."

"Where are you going?" she asked, her voice almost shaking with resentment.

"Oh, I don't know," I said casually. "I'll meet him at his office."

The military bearing in her expression changed to something less harsh, though it was by no means an "at ease," and waving her hand vaguely in my direction she went off toward the kitchen. Probably, I decided, to whisper about all this with Olga, who would agree, shaking her head ominously, that my money boded no good; that I had rich, ruinous tastes, that I would squander my money, corrupt Pritch, and then being the foolish, sunshiny young butterfly I am, would flit off, leaving them to nurse him back to health and sanity. Oh, yes, I could see it all. And they would also say, perhaps she will calm down after the precious baby comes, she's not a bad sort, just not steady and far too irresponsible.

I described all this to Bart as we had lunch—in the Drake, where we usually went, as it is near his office.

"Also, sweetie," I went on, determined to heave all of it off my chest in one sitting, "when I told her we were having lunch together today—this after my statement of financial worth had been revealed—I thought for a moment she was going up in a cloud of smoke."

This puzzled Bart. "Why, on earth? You mean you can't break bread with your own kinfolk?"

I shook my head. "Don't you see?" I said, really quite upset now that I had a chance to be. "At first she thought *I* would be paying for the lunch, and I'm sure that she thought that I wouldn't settle for anything under the price of Chambord—if she even knows what Chambord is. And I could just hear the cash register going off in her head, and her hand reaching out to snap up everything out of the till before I got a chance to throw it away. What makes people like that, Bart? Why, suddenly, does she consider me so unworthy, so foolish? It's not envy because I have more than she and all her brood could ever possibly hope for in their lives—and it's not simply that standing beside my huge pile of loot I look so small and incompetent in comparison...."

Bart sat back in his chair, speculating about it. "That's a tough one, Mole, but I know what you mean. Sometimes Ida

Bradford—and God knows they aren't poor—looks at me as if she hates me. And if there's anything really wrong between me and Joyce it is money. Because I've got so much more, it seems to make her feel inferior, and she sort of humbles herself—no, downright demeans herself—because of it, a sort of Uriah Heep act before the Golden Calf, fawning, pretending to love it, but actually just waiting for a chance to topple it over and kick it apart. You know, Mole," he fixed me with a serious look, "I'll lay you twenty to one that should something happen to me, if I died or something—"

"Bart!" I closed my hand over his in a tight grip. I couldn't bear to hear him even mention it.

"—Or even say we got a divorce and she cleaned up because of it—I'd lay you twenty to one that all this phony money-pinching routine would stop, just like that. And she'd spend it, spend it, spend it, until every dime was gone—like she was whipping it to death."

"What *makes* them that way?" I said feeling all shook up; I knew he was dead center right. "Would they like us better poor? Shall we give it all away?"

He grinned at me. "Give me yours and I'll give you mine."

"Idiot," I laughed. "No, but isn't it true that money, when you have a lot, is as much a part of your personality as your hair, or the way you laugh, or what you say and the way you say it?"

"Yes and no," he said. "You can change all those things, can't you?"

"Superficially. But aren't you a result of your past all the same, just as we are the result of Mother and Father?"

"God, Chloe, don't ask me," Bart sighed. "All I know is that people never get enough—and that people always envy anyone with great holdings, whether they be colossal Einstein brains, or musical abilities like Bach or Mozart had, or even just a dynamic personality. It makes certain people peevish, the kind who always say, 'Humph. *I* could have done that if I'd wanted to.' Or in the case of money, 'What makes her think she's so special? Just because she's so rich?' It's sort of as you said: Every time they see you, they see a great huge money sack standing right behind you, dwarfing you, because to them money is far more important than people are, I suppose. Only the very rare person—the 'big' man with the open mind—or the very rich can truly accept the very rich as simple, ordinary folk. Money is literally more trouble than it's worth, Mole—something Mother knew. Through and through."

"But what am I going to do about Pritch, Bart?" I said in consternation. "To hell with his stuffy family, but what about him? Do you think he married me for my money?"

"Of course I don't," Bart assured me, whether he meant it or not. "But I would soft-pedal the cash angle, let him pay."

"But his mother will watch every penny he spends now, and if we live beyond his allowance—and oh, Bart, it is so tiny—she'll absolutely think it's my doing, because I'm so spoiled."

"She probably will," he agreed. "But you'll just have to grit your teeth. Wait it out until you and Pritch can get away from there."

"Now you have me really worried," I said deeply troubled. "And I think maybe Pritch did take a fancy to my bank book—it was after he found out I had quite a lot that his real interest began. And then there's Lesley: *she*, even, has much more than the Allyns. How do I know he didn't just drop her and latch on to a better thing?"

"For whatever reason he dropped her, he did latch on to a better thing, Mole. You're a great girl, and you're going to be a great woman. You know I'm awfully proud of my crazy kid sister?"

"Darling," I told him, pressing his hand again.

"You and Pritch will make it," he predicted encouragingly, "just you see. I think a lot of Pritch, and I think he sees you as I do."

"I don't know," I said feeling pretty low. "You know, he really is awfully influenced by his parents, no matter what he says, and if they start hating me now—"

"Hate you? How could they—"

"Well, they might," I told him. "You see, we've sort of cheated them. I don't know what to do." And I explained then about the mock-baby; how I wasn't sure whether I had ever really been pregnant or not.

"Why in the hell didn't you tell them you weren't then?" Bart asked much perturbed. "Now they *will* think—if they want to—that there was something fishy about Pritch breaking up with Lesley and marrying you. Tell me, were they fond of Lesley?"

"I don't know, I don't know," I shook my head, feeling miserable. "Yes, I think they probably were, though they couldn't have known her terribly well. Could they have?"

He shrugged, abashed. "I don't know. Anyway, baby sister, you have got a pot of in-law stew cooking in your kitchen."

"Bart, help me," I pleaded.

"I will in every way I can, Mole, but the trouble is I don't see how I can."

"Talk to Pritch."

"I'll talk to Pritch."

"Without—without Joycie."

He sighed. "I wouldn't dream of doing otherwise these days."

"Things bad with you?"

"Not good. But they'll work. I'm patient, and besides," he grinned, "Ida Bradford, unlike your Mother Allyn, isn't making a dive—quite—for my purse strings. She's got enough money of her own to give her the strength to resist."

"God, God, money!" I sighed. "I was better off when I thought Mother was serious about leaving it to the cats and dogs."

"It works its way down to them eventually," he said, and then looked at his watch and found it was time to go back to the office.

Chapter Twelve

Pritch wouldn't look at apartments much less houses—and he wouldn't tell his parents there wasn't going to be any "precious little baby." It got more and more embarrassing: Mrs. Allyn watching my girth and diet, and the wives of Pritch's brothers spying on my shopping habits which, to their dissatisfaction, did not include Bonwit's in-waiting department, or all those lovely layette centers in the "better" stores.

We had come to a dead halt in everything, it seemed. Pritch didn't even pay sneak nocturnal visits to the guest room much anymore. And we had only been married four months. I knew he'd had a talk with Bart, but he never mentioned it, and when I asked Bart about it, he told me he had had to do all the talking. And I, feeling disloyal as hell, found I was relying more and more on Avery's friendship and counsel. Which was another thing: Pritch's mother had taken one look at Avery and had found her instantaneously poisonous. She didn't say so, of course, being such a "nice" woman, but I could tell she'd had quite a lot to say about her to Pritch who suddenly knocked her off the "good ole pal" list down to the "to-be-avoided" one. So I never brought her or her name up in that mighty fortress on the Upper West Side.

But what I really couldn't understand—and dared not pry out the explanation to—was Pritch's refusal to try to find a place of our own. He was vague at first, then irritable, bringing up the subject of money, again and again, saying he couldn't afford it, until I pointed out that he had been able to afford his flat in the Village. This brought up further unhappy details: how there were two of us now, how I was used to "certain things"—whatever this meant—how I didn't know how to "do anything." As for a reopening of our original plan to let me buy a house or a cooperative apartment—anything—that subject was as deeply buried as the gold at Fort Knox. Therefore, I knew his mother had lectured him on "self-respect" in the matter of having to cope with an heiress child-bride.

For my part, I developed a keen and well-documented revulsion for the "shabby genteel," and all their rules and ways. I hated the Christmas they made; even hated the way Father Allyn carved the turkey and the fact that they had to have turkey. I certainly loathed the sensible presents they gave me, and the odious dogged devotion to family carol-singing Christmas eve. I longed to go and throw myself on Mother's grave; beg her to let me in. "Nice" people, I learned, are just about the most vulgar in the world.

Pritch's brothers, all of whom were eons older, considered me as a sort of out-of-place and intrusive freak—yet of obvious rarity and monetary value. I was as out of place in their family circle as a piece of Tiffany glass in a hillbilly cabin. But their womenfolk, sensing that I was Tiffany, handled me with care, as well as suspicion. One and all, I know, made great sport of me behind my back, mimicked my "upper-Clahss" accent, almost openly sneered when I forgot myself and mentioned anything about my international-type upbringing, and thought I was deliberately trying to humiliate them if I confessed to having seen royalty at close quarters because my Aunt had married a baronet.

Day by day, I could see Pritch visibly twitching under the strain, and I wondered: when is he going to turn me in (or out), take me back to Tiffany's for a refund? Because it was true: I didn't fit with the rest of the house, the House of Allyn.

Avery, of course, kept saying the Allyns were just peasants, very common, but I could see that she also had never had any dealings with the middle middleclass who were a much more complicated bunch than I had ever imagined: they had all of the bad qualities of the rich and not enough of the bad qualities of the poor. They were all so Goddamn "nice" and the snobs of the world! They looked neither up nor down, but straight ahead, so all they ever saw was more of the same: more middle-class snobs, the only acceptable things to see.

The day I accidentally found an unfinished letter from Mrs. Allyn to one of her schoolgirl chums describing me as "an unprincipled child, I'm afraid, badly brought up—her table manners are simply terrible, for instance, and she has no sense of refinement, but of course her mother…" was the thing that did it. Clearly, she had bothered to inform herself completely about my background and Mother's; had checked all of our loose-lived credentials, probably in newspaper morgues, and found us uncouth and scandalous. We were just rich. I stormed around the apartment, longing to hit her. Fortunately, she was out. I cried a little, then walked the floor a little, then cried, while waiting for her to come back.

I don't know what I'd planned to tell her, but what I did tell her was that Pritch and I were moving out, pronto, into a hotel and then into the first decent house on the market, to be bought with my money—our money—since what was mine was his. And as a parting shot I told her there wasn't going to be any little baby, at least not in a few months, and she could drop her pseudo-concern for my health and let me sleep with my husband.

"Your language is disgusting," she told me coldly, and proceeded to remove her tacky hat and with great-lady type presence put it and her purse and gloves on the hall table before she turned back to deal with me. I had caught her when she was just inside the door.

"Sit down and let's have a little talk," she invited me with all the warmth of the dead fire in the fireplace.

I did so, with no particular humility, but without a word to say, as I had said it all when she came in.

She ticked off her complaint items one by one, and in all justice, the first one, at least, was just: I had only myself to blame for reading other people's mail, and, indeed, as she said, it was extremely rude of me to have done so. Then she got on to the business of our moving, pointed out their inequitable finances, when compared to mine, mentioned the danger to Pritch—and to our marriage—of making him dependent on me and turning his head with riches.

Naturally, I challenged this, told her that money never hurt anybody.

"Oh, indeed it has," she corrected me in a tone like a vise. "And I wouldn't want Pritchard to feel weakened, start moving around with a fast, irresponsible crowd, start drinking…"

I made a gesture of impatience and boredom. "Pritch is a grown man, my husband—"

"—And my son. And that's forever, Miss."

"Not if I can help it," I rose up to say. "Either you get him or I do. I'm leaving here. Tonight. Just as soon as he gets home and we can pack!"

"As you please," she inclined her head in what I suppose she thought was a poised, grand manner, befitting her "well-bredness."

"You disapproved of this marriage!" I accused her, just blazing.

"Not at first, no," she said, implacably cool.

"Whether or not," I said hotly, "it's *our* marriage—not yours!" I suddenly knew I was going to cry. "If you'll excuse me now," I said hurriedly, and made it to the guest room just in time.

After I stopped crying, I barricaded the door—a useless precaution, of course, because she couldn't have cared less. Then I sat by it, my ears tuned up like an animal's, waiting for Pritch to come home. I dashed out as soon as I heard his footsteps in the hall, and dragged him, in spite of his bewildered protests, back into the guest room.

"I've had an awful row with your mother, darling," I explained, slightly hysterical. "We've got to leave here. Now. This instant."

"Sure, Chloe," he agreed mildly, and somewhat to my surprise. "But what happened?"

As I began throwing things into suitcases—his and my things, all in a great tangle—I told him what had happened. It wasn't until I got to the baby part that I stopped for a second and thought: she had made no comment whatsoever on this. Why? But then I rushed on with my tale, while Pritch, as bidden, sat down at my extension telephone (installed and paid for by me, much to Mother Allyn's disapproval) and called the Plaza to reserve a room.

We were out of there in half an hour; out without saying good-bye. I don't even know where she was at that point. But I'm sure she knew what was going on. Probably she and Olga, two of a kind, had sneaked out of the kitchen and had had their ears pressed to the door.

Outside on the sidewalk, I took a great deep breath and reached for Pritch's hand to hold as we waited for a cab. Another mausoleum escaped from, and I could breathe again.

"Darling," I said with the utmost love when we were in the cab and on our way. "Darling."

He returned the pressure of my hand in his.

"The first thing we buy with our money is a car," I said, feeling outrageously free and wonderful with release, "and never another taxi as long as we live!"

"Not even on snowy mornings when the car won't start? Or to go and get it when it's been impounded for illegal parking?"

"No!" I laughed like an insane thing, finding it very delirious, hilariously funny, as I would have found anything he said at that moment.

It wasn't until later that I remembered it and knew it for what it was: it had absolutely spurted with sarcasm and worse, his middle-class idea that we would be reduced to street parking and other money-saving devices such as his parents and others like them employed, was hopeless proof, in all reality, of the difference in our orbits, the gulf between our private lives—past and present.

Chapter Thirteen

The house was sweet, a surprising treasure tucked away in the rear of a drab but neat little tenement on 54th Street, near Third Avenue. We found it late in the day, and it was ours by the next morning. Or mine, I should say, as that is the way it turned out.

We had been living in the Plaza for two weeks, and had rather thought we'd be going on there indefinitely as the situation looked bleak. Then we found this. Our joy was, I thought, unbounded, but that too, I soon realized, was solo. For the night of the day we signed the papers Pritch went home and never came back.

It happened this way: To my knowledge, Pritch had not communicated with his family in any way after we left, simply allowing it to be tacitly understood that he had preferred to leave with his wife. Of course, I realized later he'd probably called his mother every day, but not so then. I was, for those two weeks in the Plaza, really a bride; that was my real honeymoon, and it never occurred to me that Pritch's compliance was the docility and humoring one exhibits for a madman. I thought he was as delirious as I. Every night we did something fabulous—went to some wonderful place that the

Allyns could not possibly afford—and afterwards went to bed—together, really together—also something fabulous, and certainly something the Allyns could not, would not afford or condone. So when Pritch casually said, "Now that we have the house, I think I'd better go up and round up all my books and other junk," naturally I didn't realize he was planning to round up his marriage.

I sat in the King Cole Bar waiting for him for two hours—he had agreed to meet me there at seven—and after four answerless phone calls to the Allyn's house, I finally got the pitch. They were deliberately not answering the phone; Pritch had deliberately ditched me. I called Avery, luckily found her at home, and after she came down to join me in my widow-wake we both proceeded to get so roaring drunk that they didn't even want to serve us dinner at the little place we finally ended up.

During dinner, I kept getting up, staggering to the phone to call our hotel room; I did this until the switchboard operator impatiently cut me off because she couldn't understand what I was saying.

"No use, no use, no use," I told Avery, and put my head down on the red-checkered cloth of our table and cried until it was drenched. The next day I woke up in Avery's apartment.

Hungover as a Babylonian garden, I made plans, having persuaded Avery to skip a day at work. I'd move into the house and wait.

She looked at me commiseratingly, but with all the sadness with which one views the hopeless. Finally I asked her to give me her version of it.

"I don't want to," she said rather nervously. "It will—or may—just make you hate me later."

"Do," I pleaded, counting on her, wondering what I would ever do without her.

"To begin with," she said. "I don't think he consciously planned to walk out, but once you had the house—a place for you to lay your head, a place of your own—I think he felt his responsibility considerably lightened—*i.e.*, he could consider other aspects of the thing, and was therefore more receptive to his parents' views."

"Which were?" I interrupted.

"Obvious." She made a gesture. "I'm sure, for instance, that Mrs. Allyn brought up the subject of the non-baby as soon as he hit home."

"Probably," I agreed morosely. "But would he really let her talk him into believing that I'd tricked him into marriage, or that he had married me solely because I needed to be made into an honest woman?"

"You're way out in front, Chloe," she said quietly. "It's nothing we can really know. Anything could have happened. Maybe it wasn't mentioned at all."

"Call the Plaza again for me, will you?"

With a resigned look, she did, but just as both of us knew, there was no answer. "How about calling him at Columbia?" she suggested.

I told her it was too complicated; I didn't even know his class schedule.

"Send him a wire, then. At home."

"I could, I suppose," I said slowly, then I began to consider the whole thing: why should I? He knew where I was, he knew what this would do to me. If he had wanted to be with me, he would have been. "No, Avery," I said at last. "I'll just move into the house and wait."

"You can't live all alone there!" she exclaimed.

"I don't intend to," I answered. "First, I'll send for Tennie and Jess—there's lots of room for them, there's the whole fourth floor—then if he hasn't turned up in a month, you're moving in with me. Absolutely. Don't say a word."

And she didn't say a word, that sweet wise friend, and a month later in she moved.

I must say those first few weeks we lived together in that house, snug, secure, with Tennie and Jess upstairs to watch over us, and we evening after evening downstairs in the living room reading by the fire, or watching TV, or just talking, were serene evenings, but for the fact that I was inside as furrowed as a plowed field, each gaping crevice a mortally bleeding wound of misery. The silent telephone was like a black Frankenstein's monster I could not bring to life. And when I say silent, I mean silent, for no one called either of us, except occasionally Bart, or sometimes a wrong number. And when that happened I jumped like a startled insect.

Avery somehow had managed to keep it out of her paper that Pritch and I were pfftt, as they call it, and since hers was more or less the mouthpiece for such delicacies, no one else had dug up the news. I led in those days such a discreetly quiet life that it was tantamount to a silent life. In the daytime,

I watched Tennie cook and clean, or went out furniture shopping, or went to awful grade B movies by myself. Then home for dinner, which was always blessedly Tennie-good, and Avery, then bed. I had bought a car, and Jess drove me around whenever I wanted, which was most of the time, for I was too nervous and unhappy to cope with daytime city traffic myself.

I don't know whose idea it was to shift from low-gear into something higher and slightly faster, but I know it was about the time that I got a legal separation from Pritch, pursuant to an annulment, if possible, and if not, an out-of-state quick divorce.

Anyway, Avery and I decided to go out for drinks and dinner for a change, and she declared herself irresistibly drawn to the Village.

"Memories," I said. "Ghosts."

"Cut them," she said. "Just as you would human beings. It's got to be done, Chloe."

I knew she was right, and I headed us in the car downtown toward the Village.

Still, I would have given a lot to have known what went on sub rosa between Pritch and Mother Allyn those two weeks we lived so happily apart from them at the Plaza; but more, I would have bought my soul back from the Devil to have known what went on *the* night, the last one I saw him. The lawyer, of course, had spoken to Pritch and seemed rather embarrassed by the whole thing. But this much I gathered: Pritch's excuse for breaking up with Lesley and marrying me was that I was pregnant. Somehow going through the legal bit of shearing him was easier after that example of callow cowardliness. From now on he would always be "Brother" Allyn to me, Mrs. New England Allyn's little boy.

Avery tried to rouse me—oh, she did every day. She almost pinched my cheeks, but I would not come back to life. Mostly because I didn't know where life had gone. And I would think: Avery, Dear Muchness: You deserve a rollicking not a sobersides companion. But there we were, curiously stuck together on a small desert island called Manhattan's Upper East Side. We sent up occasional flares; went out on occasional exploratory tours; the trip to the Village was one of them.

We were there—Fifth Avenue and Eight Street—and the question occurred to us simultaneously: now that we're here, what?

We decided to park the car, and we both concentrated intently on this problem, like seamstresses over knots in thread. Then when it was parked, Avery said again, "Now, what?"

"Food," was all I could suggest, and we made for one of the fine Village restaurants where we ate a good and tasty dinner which neither of us tasted.

We hardly spoke, but on the other hand, we didn't look around either. All of our hundred-horsepower drive had just faded like fog, and we blinked at each other, each thinking, let's go home, but neither wanting to admit the drizzle of it all.

The check paid, coats put on, we were again outside, in the street. Avery looked up at the streetlights, which shed so much light on so many strangers, interesting-looking strangers, like a child staring at the distant glow of a carnival. "What's wrong with us," she murmured sadly—rhetorically—then asked me where we'd parked the car.

"On Waverly, I think," I said, heading down MacDougall Street.

"Shall we go home? It seems so alive down here somehow…."

I was just ready to say it didn't, when up he strode, Seymour—Seymour whatever his name was, the one we had met with Pritch, months ago.

"Well!" he said heartily. "Hello, there, you two up-towners." He beamed at us some more, sort of "raring" back on his heels, his hands stuck in the pockets of a worn-out Navy peajacket. I noticed he had terribly bad teeth, even there in the lamplight, and that his beard was worn pointed now, like a Satan's.

We murmured cool hellos, quiet and subterranean as an underground stream; both of us wanted to cut out. Faced with this character again, I remembered he had smelled like stale bedclothes.

"Saw Pritch the other day," he went on, apparently hugely enjoying this confrontation. Or maybe he was just being friendly, and wasn't ribbing us.

"Oh?" I said, non-committedly, and felt Avery nudge me to break it up, move on.

But Seymour barred the way. "Where you dolls headed?"

I made an empty gesture, and he said, "How about a cup of coffee?"

Personally, I didn't want to be rude, nasty as I considered this bearded genius, but I certainly didn't want coffee either. My momentary hesitation seemed to encourage him and with another ingratiating smile, he went to work on Avery. "New espresso place just opened up down the street. The most. Having a show of pix by a friend of mine. Great girl. From the Coast. Great art. Very beat—"

"What do you mean, 'very beat'?" Avery put in, bristling strangely, it seemed to me, at this rather innocuous person.

"Beatific! The most!" he went on extolling, and it occurred to me that the reason he was as joyous as hell was that he was high on marijuana, as he had been previously, and probably was most of the time.

I looked at Avery, to see if she shared my slight disgust and strong urge to part company with this type, but she was looking fascinated. He was now talking about Photography, with a capital P, and how his West Coast friend stacked up beside the other greats—Walker, Stieglitz, Cartier-Bresson.

"Come on, let's do go see!" Avery urged me, impulsively. Just one look at her told me she was sold. I hadn't seen her light up that way since immediately after her graduation from Miss Chalmers' when she had embraced me and everybody wildly shrieking, "I'm OUT!" How right she was; she was very far out, which had nothing to do with being free, and now she was OUT even further.

Anyway, the three of us headed for the coffee house-gallery, Avery and this Seymour person walking slightly ahead, talking very fast and enthusiastically—or rather he was, and she was listening at the same rate of speed. She couldn't take her eyes off him. I wondered if they'd even know it, if I simply hung back and disappeared. I was very tempted.

Chapter Fourteen

Seymour, it appeared, knew even less of our names than we knew of his. Avery's name—Avery Stafford—didn't seem to make any particular impression on him, but mine really threw him. "Chloe Longtree!" he chortled, throwing his head back for another good, rich laugh. "What a name!"

Avery gave him a look as sour as penicillin. Now, I suppose, she was sorry she hadn't introduced me as Chloe Allyn, which, of course, I legally was, but for some devious reason she had decided that Seymour didn't know Pritch and I were married, that he might "tell us something" if we played it quiet and cool, and God knows what other ideas for machinations and intrigue she had in mind. But that was the way Avery was. Open up her tiny little mind, I always said, and inside you'd find a tiny cloak and a tiny dagger—all very harmless, but sometimes tiresomely complicated, as for instance now. Moreover, I hadn't the faintest idea why *she* resented his mirthful reaction to my name; I was the injured party, but was quite used to it, could handle the situation myself. But I didn't get a chance; she was in and at 'em.

"You're something of a humorist, aren't you?" she asked, sarcasm dripping from her tongue, her face as benign as a puff adder's. In fact I was somewhat surprised by it all; it had happened so fast.

Seymour, however, rose to the occasion, recognizing the mating call of competitiveness, and there was much dialogue and much flashing of the eyes between them. He first defended his wit, then his honorable name (which was Marlboro, and sounded very borrowed and made up) and then went into his tortured, sensitive background. I still hadn't had a chance to say a word in defense of the time-honored Longtrees or to smite him across the face with my gauntlet, as I would have gladly done. "—And furthermore, my mother was a poet and a musician—a great musician—with music in her soul," he told Avery, all choked up "—you silly square rich dames don't know anything about people like that—"

"We do now," Avery said drily. "You've just told us."

He ignored her. "—every word she said was a poem, every gesture she made was pure music—"

"Jazz," Avery put in. "Primitive."

But he didn't hear this either; didn't hear me snicker, or see Avery's broad grin. I guess he really was pretty high. His eyes certainly looked it.

Suddenly he groped for, grabbed and held Avery's hand, in a sort of Indian wrestler's deadlock. "—You, you," he told her throatily diving into and drowning in her eyes, "—you could be—you're so beautiful, white, blonde, shining like a goddess—" then he dropped her hand abruptly, as if she had forced a very hot potato on him when he wasn't looking "—but you're dead inside. DEAD! What do you know of the magic of childhood? The sweetness of the mornings, the gold hot noons, The summer-tangled streets of kids at play?"

"With Hoola hoops," Avery again interjected. I couldn't stand it. Both of us were giggling like fools now, and I didn't want to laugh out loud in his poor blind face, so intense now that it was almost incandescent.

"I'm going to look at these famous photographs," I whispered to Avery, getting up to wander off.

My departure, I noticed, received all the fanfare and attention of a pebble cast into a brook, and Avery, for all her wisecracking, was really glued to his side, like a lovely dragon fly next to the house variety on a piece of flypaper. Or so it appeared from here. I scanned the photographs perfunctorily. They were mediocre, as I'd expected, impressive only to those who had a personal concern for the lady who took the pictures, or for those who had never seen any others. The only salient message they had was that the lady had traveled widely, had a good camera, and had used a lot of film up while crouched in some peculiar positions herself.

Through with that exhibition, I turned back to the other: Avery was still in a state of enchantment, despite her amusing asides which she was now delivering to herself or still into his deaf ear. I looked at her, elbows on the table, chin cupped in her short, graceful hands, a bemused expression on her face; yes, she was still being desperately defensive—or offensive— but she was a goner and her rapier of wit was made out of rubber. For he sat, self-satisfied as ever, tuned into himself, the volume way up and blaring, looking incongruously young and pathetic but awful for all his genius-style affectations; the blue-jean encased legs languidly twined around the legs of the adjoining chair (mine), his hands dropped off behind his own chair looking like a pair of big gloves hung up to dry. His head was cocked just-so, and occasionally he shifted his health-club type manly torso, and occasionally, without taking his large dark eyes—hot, passionate eyes—off Avery's face, he reached up to stroke his beard, as fondly as if it were a pet cat. I didn't even wonder what they were saying. Instead, I shuddered.

When I hovered over the table, feeling very much like an embarrassed guardian angel, I saw I would have to do more than just that: now, they *both* ignored me.

"Man, that's the message!" he was saying, in answer, I presume, to some faultless observation Avery had made.

"Let's go, Avery," I said roughly, as if I were rousing her from a sound sleep. But it needed more than that.

"So," she said, in the soft voice of someone drugged, "I got with it—for the first time—and I knew what Coleridge felt, what Macaulay meant, and why Modigliani started to paint the way he did."

"Say!" he exclaimed suddenly, looking up at me with those orbs of his instantly burning away my frosty objectivity. "This is a *great* girl! She knows everything. Chloe—" he grabbed my arm as if he were yanking on a stage-curtain pull. "Sit down! Listen! This girl's the *greatest!*"

And I was rung down, into my previous seat, and bent my absorption to theirs. The interest between them crackled like Fourth-of-July fireworks. But it was hard to wedge in the cold steel needle of coherence, so I sat back and took in the conversation as the words flew.

Eventually, I gathered Avery was confessing all: to wit, that she too had been "turned on" and thought marijuana great. I know that earlier in the evening, I would have found this piece of autobiography pulse-raising, but now I took it as I would have an unusual maneuver from a tennis player during an exciting match. I kept turning my head from side to side. They were both unreal and brilliant, playing a game. Soon it would all be over and we would be going home. But then, I realized, they were planning something further. Avery said fervently, or swore fervently, that she wanted to "turn on"—yes, tonight. Not in his pad—not in ours (how did "ours" get into this?)—but he knew *the* place. Not very far uptown, no, past Chelsea. Not the Puerto Rican section, either—we'd see—he didn't want to say anything, we'd see for ourselves—it was the greatest—

"We've got the car," Avery said, sounding drunk though she hadn't had a drop. "It'll be easy."

And before I could believe it, we were out of the place— Avery had taken care of the check—and this Seymour person talking, talking all the while, way above fever-pitch with intensity, was helping me toward my own automobile as if I were too inebriated to stand up and make it on my own.

I got in, feeling numb, and he told me where to go. I started the car, noticing the way he and Avery melted together, their hands interlocked in another death-do-us-part grip, their eyes having a mutual feast. And I marveled on the Seymour energy—drug inspired, or not—he was like a walking atomic pile, and all of its life force was bent on Love—

love for everybody—Brotherhood of Man. He would have even picked up the Ancient Mariner, I decided. Which made his finding Avery a superb piece of serendipity indeed. About that time, he even put his arm around me; gave me a good squeeze which almost made me sideswipe a car. But his real attention was drawn to Avery, and they trained eyes upon each other as intently as those electrical ones that open doors. Or move worlds. I drove where I was told, also semi-bewitched, I suppose.

On the West Side, in the midst of all those printing companies, I found the address. All by myself, for by that time Avery and Seymour were deep in the oozing marshes and quicksands of lovemaking, and I felt embarrassed to be around at all—but sort of bewitched, as I say, their spell cast over me. Anyway, I saw, as I gave a quick nervous look, it could still sneak under the heading of necking, what they were doing, so it was all right to say, "We're here." Which is what I said.

"Briefing period," said Seymour, straightening up, swallowing hard, and trying to sound composed, though hoarse. "It's on the top floor. The password is S.K.S. and you're going to find a lot of people high on the weed, in the nude, and swinging."

I must have made some noise of incredulity, for Avery wound herself out of her clench enough to say, "Honey, stay with it," which was hardly enough of an encouragement.

However, we mounted the stairs, those two ahead, holding onto each other, clasped, like fleeing refugees, or lovers in the Dore illustrated Dante's *Inferno*. I followed, landing after landing, some bearing the names of commercial enterprises with arrows pointed toward their doors, or artists' signs, artily done, welcoming guests (invited ones, of course, as the uninvited would never find their way here) or silent landings where nothing proclaimed, except dirt and stillness, and the slanted stair-rails, ancient creaking floors, and the accumulated dirt of the industrial age. And at last we came to a violently violet-colored door initialed S.K.S., all in gold leaf and English-Gothic lettering. Seymour lurched forward and knocked.

Then the door opened.

Completely nude before us stood our host. I think the thing that shocked me most was his crew cut, and the vague impression that in his clothes I would have recognized him, at least, from somewhere else. However, he looked us up and down, and then he said, "Who are you?"

"We're looking for Shelley," Seymour cried, his voice almost piteous. "He *told* us to come."

S.K.S., or whoever he was, stared at us again; but already I had learned the signs: marijuana governed his vision—or visions—and with an almost sightless look, we were admitted, he making a slight obeisance from the waist, as if he were drunk and entertaining in Newport. Newport! That's what did it. "Isn't that Sonny Saunders?" I tried to whisper in Avery's ear, but her ear was out of earshot. Instead, I found myself confiding in the ear of our host.

He merely looked at me, his eyes were as unanimated as before, but something else had come into them as he gazed at me, as if I were a voluptuous Petty Girl, and he half-snarled, half Mae-West-insinuated, "Take off your clothes."

I looked back at this S.K.S. very sharply. "What if I don't?" I said.

"Then you leave," he pronounced tersely. "Your friends are taking off their clothes. Either you do or you leave."

"What are you besides a host, Sonny?" I asked. "Are you God?"

If he heard the "Sonny," part he didn't take note or umbrage, but the "God" reference threw him into a rage. Suddenly, I found myself in a roomful of people—where he had deliberately pushed me—seemingly to be stoned—who were all obviously his devout followers, judging by the way they looked up at him, in the most worshipful attitudes, as if he were the Heavenly Father. Their expressions while full of awe, reverence, and yes, beatitude (the Beat Generation), held something else which distinguished them from the case-book religious fanatic: the glaze in their eyes wasn't the simple transport of ecstasy, but the frozen-pupil stare of the drugged: they were all sky-high on pot, and all stark naked. They lay around that room—which was completely bare except for a hi-fi moaning out an African recording—lolling on the thick wall-to-wall carpeting looking like statues just uncrated for the Whitney collection. And it was bitter cold too, so cold that the blue of the marijuana smoke which stood in thick clouds, as still as the user's eyes, seemed an atmospheric stage effect.

I looked up at Sonny Saunders—S.K.S., and/or God—and wondered if he was going to turn his pack loose on me, bid them to tear me apart, or at least unclothe me, and saw that instead of throwing me to the wolves, he was giving them some other sign to which they gave their hushed-breath attention.

Shades of Aleister Crowley! I looked at him incredulously and for a fraction of a second felt drawn into his piercing eye like a thread drawn into a needle, powerless under his hypnotism. Then common sense whispered: this is just Sonny Saunders who once broke your tennis racket out at Glen Cove; the same Sonny Saunders with the funny crew-cut who was at what's-her-name's dinner party in Newport—only then he had on clothes, dinner clothes at that.

"Come off it, Sonny," I told him, hoping I sounded casual. "Remember me?" I went on, a little short of breath, "I knew you before you were deified." I tried to smile. But this was no time for levity, his expression clearly told me, and I felt like an Aztec sacrificial offering trying to joke the high-priest executioner out of it all.

"You will be dealt with," he promised in a trancelike sepulchral voice.

"All right, I'll leave," I answered. "I just want to collect the people I came with—at least Avery Stafford—" And suddenly I was talking to myself. He had simply disappeared, probably into a cloud of marijuana smoke.

Futilely, I looked about for a place to sit down, but there simply wasn't any except the floor, so instead I edged over by the nearest exit, and stood against the wall, my eyes beginning to sting as I scrutinized the crowd, looking for some sign of Avery and that fantastic creature who had brought us here.

Suddenly in the moiling mob, I saw Avery's albino-white

shock of hair, blending with Seymour's. And with spotting Avery in this snakepit, reality came thundering down upon me like an avalanche. I turned physically sick with disgust, humming with hurt, outrage, and compassion all at once, so that I was like a dynamo of unbearable conflicting feeling, and I flung myself at the door, and tore it open.

Chapter Fifteen

That's where Sonny Saunders took over. He was just on the other side of the door, standing by the tallest, biggest, most biceped male I've ever seen. Sonny didn't say a word, simply jerked his head in my direction. And Atlas lifted me off my feet, as if I weighed no more than his own hand, and carried me down a hall. I'm sure I screamed, and I'm sure I fought him, but it was like Fay Wray in the clutches of King Kong.

If I had visions—and I had—of being raped, brutally, voluptuously, or any which way, I was wrong; Hercules simply deposited me outside the violet-colored front door, closed it in my startled face, and left me in the crashing silence that always follows a terrible din. I guess I pounded on it for a while, then I sat down and had hysterics on the filthy, littered top step of the long staircase.

I was sobbing, talking out loud to myself, I know, giving me a scathing lecture. How-did-I-get-into-this? it probably ran. Then I heard an answer.

"How did you get into this? You asked for it," a man's voice said crisply. I looked up. I was blocking the way of one of the few unbearded, dressed (in a business suit) older men

I had seen that night.

"I'm sorry," I moaned, inching over to give him room to pass. And he passed, but at the door he said, "Want to come back inside?"

I shook my head miserably.

"Well, then," he said in the same crisp voice, "adios."

And that was the end of him. I heard the door shut, and I was left again in the cold, dusty silence of the old warehouse building with only my own noises of misery to keep me company.

Finally, my own personal dawn began to come out of the pitch blackness of my hysteria. I scrambled to my feet. If Avery wanted—wanted what was back there, okay! I didn't. I began to run down the steps, and then I heard a deep, booming male voice echoing down the stairwell. "Chloe Longtree!" it sounded. "Chloe Longtree!"

I slowed down and looked up, and there was this same man who had passed me on the stairs. I waited. I could hear him rapidly coming down. "Wait!" he called again, as if he thought I wouldn't.

Clutching the stair rail where I stood, I watched him round the last landing and approach me. There was a tentative smile on his face, not eager or polite, but rather like a salesman's. "You *are* Chloe Longtree?" he asked rhetorically and added, "Incredible name. Was it changed from Grossbaum?"

"No," I said, my voice still small and slightly withered from the trauma of all this. "I don't think so."

"Lovely name anyway," he went on, but with no oily

smile, thank God. Just an observation. "You think you can find your way out of this rat trap?"

"I'm sure I can," I said stonily, and started back downstairs.

But he was right behind me, as if I had said no. "Your girl friend sent me to find you," he said chattily. "I'm Shelley. Shelley Spivak."

And with that I turned on him. "Then you must be a monster! It's because of you that my 'girl friend'—as you call her—and I got into this!"

He looked at me coldly, as if I were an illogical, hot-headed fool. Then he shrugged his shoulders. "I could say that water seeks its own level."

"Please don't!" I yelled at him imperiously, and started down the stairs again, my heels pounding out my indignation. Still, in the background, I could hear him following me.

At the bottom of the stairs, he grabbed me by the elbows. "You're the most hard-bitten, peevish teenager I've ever seen," he informed me.

I slapped him in the face. "Go upstairs to your gutter!"

Then he slapped me back. "That's precisely what I intend to do after I put you in your expensive little foreign car and head you on your way, out of harm's way."

"Don't bother!" I advised him, longing to put a hand to my red, stinging face.

For an answer, he took my arm and skillfully projected me like a guided missile through the outer door. "Now where's your car?" he asked firmly.

We were on the stoop, and very carefully, I undid his fingers from my arm, as if they were a string of band-aids. "I told you," I said in a level voice, "that I don't want your help. And I'll tell you why: I have no business in a place like that. And my friend has none. We were persuaded here so your odious friend could meet you. Because of it, my friend apparently took leave of her senses. I can't help that. I'm going. I can find my way, and I prefer to find it alone. Clear?"

He had eyes as hard as, as cold as, and the color of agates. They bored into me. Rather like S.K.S.'s had, only Shelley Spivak's were like a clear winter day, full of sharpness, completely aware and keen. "Are you finished?" he asked.

But he could see by my face that I was. Completely. I hoped I would not sob; to throw myself on his sympathy was like seeking succor from the Great Stone Face. "Now, where is your car?" he asked, his voice as quiet as a library, and as thoughtful.

We got to it. I fumbled with the keys to unlock it. He took them from my hand and expertly opened the door himself. He handed me in, and when I started to slide toward the driver's seat, he said, "Ahh-ahh," indicating that he proposed to occupy that himself. In a minute he was at the other door, and I found myself obliging him by turning up the door handle inside, unlocking it, so he could get in. He did, and we stared at each other wordlessly for a few minutes. Then he said: "Sy Marlboro is a fool."

I nodded. "And a dangerous one."

"That depends," he said thoughtfully. "But he's no judge of people. That other girl, all right, but not you."

"I guess he thought he had to take me along to get her," I said wistfully.

"He didn't think at all," he corrected me, his voice crisp to harshness again.

I studied him in the half light. He seemed to be about twenty-eight or so, older than Bart. And completely different. He had rich lustrous hair, curly and oily, or at least oiled. And in profile he looked something like a handsome bird or an extinct wild animal, or a wild man from a curious long-dead race—an Assyrian, or a Hittite. He had the long curved Semitic nose, the full sensual mouth, the high brow of the long-vanished, once proud over-civilized but savage people who had first inhabited the earth. I thought about saying so, so fascinated I was by what I saw, but one lesson I had learned tonight was CAUTION. However, he was really very beautiful in a foreign kind of way, and I was now, quietened, grateful to him for his clinical kindness to me. I had needed some human company after that experience. But then, I reminded myself, he was in some way closely connected with all that madness. I asked him, without any preface, just how.

He didn't seem surprised at my abruptness at all.

"Oh, I turn on occasionally," he said. "I like it better than alcohol for escape. Much cleaner. Actually, I prefer real hashish—pot is just for kids."

I considered this calm statement of his: its softness was like a blanket drawn over the body of a mangled corpse. Was he unaware of the corpse, how it got that way? Or was he just philosophical about it? "You shock me," I told him in a low, shaken voice.

"I do?" he turned to me swiftly. "That's not surprising. I expect you'd be rather shocked by the Easter Islanders—Maoris—or any peoples whose customs were not yours."

"That's true," I admitted, my voice smaller than ever. I was thinking how Pritch's family, and their folkways, had shocked me, and they were a tribe to be found next to my elbow, under my nose, and had been all my life. "You see, I'm not very old," I added lamely.

His laugh was instantaneous, appreciative; a pure delight. "At least you know it," he said. "That's more than most of those people up there know."

I agreed, then told him about Sonny Saunders, how I'd known him slightly all my life.

He gave a long, low whistle of surprise. "Well, I'll be damned!" he said profoundly, sounding as if he would. "I knew the kid had plenty of loot, but I didn't know he was an escapee from the Four Hundred."

"He isn't exactly," I put in uncomfortably, ready to go into a very complicated explanation of Sonny's background—how he was in, but *not* in—but face value was enough for Shelley Spivak. He chortled and glowed over this "find" like an archaeologist with a priceless treasure. Then he said to me, "If you know all this about S.K., that means *you're* one of those crazy-rich too-much-too-often dolls. You writing a book about it?"

I laughed uneasily. "The idea has crossed my mind."

"It has certainly crossed mine," he said. "As a matter of fact, I am a writer of sorts. Edited the college paper out on the Coast, got mixed up with the poetry-jazz set—that's how

I know our friend Seymour—and then I worked on a news-paper here in New York. Till I got canned for goldbricking. It was a lousy job anyway."

"What are you doing now?"

"Looking for another job to goldbrick on."

"But if you want to write why don't you like such jobs?"

He laughed at me again, and told me it wasn't the same thing. "I'm a *real* writer," he explained, "not just a plodding reporter type with big ears and a sharp pencil."

"Oh. You mean you're interested in real journalism—Rebecca West, people like that," I said, pulling a name out of the air.

"Yeah, that's the pitch," he looked at me with interest. "Which brings us back to your original question: how I figure in all that stuff upstairs. I don't. I'm just a guilty bystander, one of the few His Holiness allows to stay fully clothed in that unheated marijuana den he calls the 'Sacred Sanctum,' or the 'Temple.' I first heard about him when he tried to make a case for the legalized use of narcotics by having himself committed to Bellevue. It was in all the papers. Didn't you see it?"

"No," I said. "I guess I was still in England." I wondered if I should go on to tell him that I was married too, but he just looked interested, said, "oh, really?" and went on enthu-siastically giving me an account of Sonny's activities.

"He interests me," he said. "I'd like to do a story on him."

I agreed Sonny's efforts were courageous if a little outrageous.

"Outrageous? He's completely mad," Shelley corrected

me. "However, you have to give the guy credit He's got a point in sticking up for pot. It should be on the open market. It's the perfect opiate for the people, so to speak. And God knows they've got to have something. Nobody can live very long in this goofed-up society without some kind of reliable anodyne."

I thought about this for a while, and was still wondering whether he was as right as he sounded, when he said, "Well, kid. You all right now? Think you can make it home?"

It rather took me aback; I don't know what I thought, but sitting there, talking to him—or hearing him talk—I'd completely lost track of the facts involved, and certainly of the obvious one that I had originally thought of him as a monster; now he was like a very close and very wise older friend. "I can make it," I told him.

He got out of my car, his long legs gracefully, skillfully avoided the hazards of the steering wheel and gear shift. He slammed the door, smiled inside and said, "So long now!"

"So long!" I called back and watched him stride up the street, back to the veritable den of iniquity where he was observer and Chief Scribe.

Chapter Sixteen

When I heard the front door open the next morning, I was still in bed. Avery, at last, I thought to myself, and turned over, pulling one pillow up over my head, and settling another under it, making, as Avery called it, a pillow sandwich. Then the next thing I knew, Tennie was tentatively saying from the doorway of my room, "Miss Chloe? They's some man downstairs."

"What?" I asked and shot to an upright position. "Who? What is it?"

"He didn't say what he wants. Just said he'd come to see you."

"All right," I told her, my heart having dropped down like an elevator to the bottom of its shaft. And I got up and quickly threw on the first clothes I saw. Probably a plain-clothesman, I thought. They'd raided that horrible place, taken Avery in, and she was now probably in the Women's Detention Home. Oh, the damned desperate fool! Why couldn't she, as Mother always said, stick with people of her own sort?

I hurried downstairs, and there in the living room, grinning up at me, as comfortably at home as a cat, was one

Shelley Spivak.

"Hi!" he called genially. "I was in the neighborhood. Just thought I'd drop in."

I stopped and stared at him. "I didn't hear you knock."

"I didn't knock," he said, as if he thought me crazy for imagining he would. "I tried the door and it wasn't locked, so I just walked in."

That subject dismissed, and without further ado, he marched around the room, looking at everything. "Nice place you've got here. That fireplace work?"

I told him it did.

"Good taste too," he added. "Yours? Or maybe some decorator's?"

"Mine."

"You're a pretty bright doll to be so young," he commented, giving me a sidewise look, as if I were an *objet d'art* up for appraisal. "I thought you'd live in one of those artsy-craftsy pads, all Japanese, no individuality, somebody else's idea—but this isn't too bad at all. Family stuff?" he asked, fingering a very rare piece of Meissen.

"No," I said quite coldly. I still hadn't asked him to sit down, and had not yet decided whether or not I should. "How did you get my address?"

"Your girl friend," he said casually. "She asked me to drop around."

"Why couldn't she have come herself, or telephoned?"

He laughed at me, his humor lazy, somewhat mocking. "She's in no condition, and anyway she's shacked up with Sy and he doesn't have a telephone anymore."

At that news, *I* sat down.

"Don't get all excited," Shelley Spivak said. "It's not as bad as that, kid. She'll be all right."

I shook my head, too worried to say anything.

"Cheer up," he went on encouragingly. "Nothing's going to happen to her."

"It's all so awful," I murmured.

"Not at all," he corrected me with ease. "Sy's not a bad fellow."

I shuddered and he saw me.

"No, he's a little stupid and a little eager, which makes him reckless, but essentially he's all right."

"The whole thing is simply terrible," I said limply. "I should never have left her there."

"Probably not," he agreed, "but you didn't have much choice, now did you? Anyway, kid, I'll look after her. I made her try to remember where you lived so I could come tell you not to worry about her. She couldn't remember your phone number though. That's why I came personally."

"Thank you," I said dimly. "That was very nice of you."

"Not at all," he said heartily.

Somewhere in all this, he had sat down at the other end of the couch. Now he got up. "Well, I'll be going," he announced.

I stood up. "Why don't you stay and have some coffee? Or breakfast? I just got up and haven't had any."

"No, no thanks!" he said good-humoredly, giving me a warm fraternal-like smile. "I'm pavement pounding today—and I've got to go to the library sometime, and look up some stuff on this narcotic law that S.K. is trying to buck—I'm working with him and a couple of doctors researching this thing, to see if we can find some way to bust it—"

I thought it sounded admirable. Crude as this man obviously was, he had both gentleness and intelligence. "How can I help Avery, get her out of this?" I asked seriously.

"Leave her alone. It'll do her good," he advised. "She'll come back in a few days."

I shook my head, feeling very old-fashioned—like her grandmother—but firm. "I'm not trying to be her protector, really," I explained. "But I think she should come back—now."

"I'm afraid she won't do that," Shelley smiled. "I've already talked to her about it."

"Maybe she would listen to me—if I could just talk to her—"

"That's simple," he said as pleasant and calm as a social worker. "Got a pencil and paper handy? I'll give you the address."

I took it down—an address in the west part of the Village, a section I didn't know at all. "How do I get there?" I asked, and he gave me the directions, very complicated-sounding.

He noticed my bewildered stare as I looked at my notes and said, "If you're not in any hurry I could meet you somewhere and drive you down later—say about five o'clock."

I readily agreed; I didn't relish driving down there alone in any event, and on this particular errand. "Why don't we meet at the King Cole at five?" I suggested.

"Where's that?" he asked.

Faintly surprised that he didn't know, I told him. But he shook his head. "None of your fancy joints for me," he said. "I'm a peasant, and when I go to a bar it's got to be a first cousin to an old-fashioned saloon. Anyway, I don't drink anymore, so why make it a bar? How's Macy's instead!"

"Macy's!" I gasped.

"Not inside," he told me. "Just at the entrance, my favorite one. You can't miss it. They've got a plaque commemorating the Straus couple who went down on the *Titanic*, and under it is this corny poem in a frame all about 'Sara' and how 'up she is holding her husband'—or something like that. Very dialectical. You can almost hear Mrs. Nussbaum reading it."

"Are you an anti-Semite?" I asked. I had heard that some Jews were and found it very strange.

"No. I'm just a Jew with a sense of humor. Don't you like jokes about old-line one hundred per cent two-headed, red-blooded Americans?"

"I never heard any."

This brought on another faint explosive blast of laughter. "You are certainly one cool nowhere doll," he informed me, but added, "however, I like it. I like you." He looked at me quite seriously. Then he made a slight bow, walked to the front door, as familiar with its location as though it were his, said, "Good morning, Miss Chloe Longtree," and was gone.

I heard Tennie coming up from the kitchen, panting as she came. She and Jess aren't young anymore. "Who in the name of the Lord was that?" she cried out at me.

"Hard to explain," I said. "Where's my breakfast?"

"Downstairs. Where'd you think it was at? And what's happened to Miss Stafford? Is she gone off and got herself into trouble with the likes of him?"

"Now, Tennie," I calmed her. "Avery's all right Just keep your shirt on."

This made her furious. "Don't you go worryin' about my shirt, Miss You! You better be worryin' about yours! You and that Miss Stafford is two of the craziest young 'uns I ever seen in my life! Miss Cornelia must of lost her mind there at the end to leave you all that money where you could jus' dip in and help yourself any old time before you was old enough to—"

"Now, hush, Tennie," I said, quite annoyed myself.

"I won't hush a-tall. I'm gonna call Mr. Bart, that's what I'm going to do!"

"I haven't done a *thing*, Tennie," I insisted. "Now look at me. Don't I look perfectly all right?"

"You looks all right, but you ain't!" Tennie said emphatically, then she went on to grumble about Pritch, and what were they making young gentlemen out of these days anyway?

I told her I certainly didn't know, couldn't care less, and would she please give me some breakfast.

She did, but she called Bart anyway.

He turned up about noon, looking like a priest come to administer extreme unction. He made me tell him all about it. I did, doing a skillful editing job on most of the night before, but admitted we had been to a rather wild party and that

Avery had gone off with somebody.

I didn't reassure him at all somehow; he couldn't have looked more worried. "I don't know what to say to you, Mole." He shook his head. "Sometimes you seem so much older than you really are, but then at other times—like now—I feel you don't know what you're doing. Your sense is all right, but your experience isn't. You just don't know what you're up against with people of that sort. You've got no frame of reference. I'm sure they're interesting, intelligent, sensitive, stimulating—"

"They don't shape up all that great," I interjected, "I'm not going 'Village.'"

"You sure?"

"Positive," I said. "I find all that bit a little revolting."

He didn't look as convinced as I would have liked. "I can't tell you what to do," he said again. "But I worry plenty. By the way, any news of Pritch?"

I shook my head, that old lost, terrible feeling suddenly drowning me.

"He was all wrong for you, anyway. Very weak. Immature. Might have worked out a few years from now, but he didn't seem to know what he wanted. Kept changing his mind. A real faddist."

I perked up my ears. "Have you seen him?"

Bart shook his head. "Not once."

"You sound as if you had—or heard from him, or something."

"Indirectly, only. Ida was in to see us the other day. Seems he's been calling Lesley."

"When are they publishing the bans?" I asked bitterly.

"Now, Mole, be sensible. You don't think Lesley would go along with any reconciliation at this point, do you?"

"Of course I do!" I stormed. "Anyway, I don't care! I made a mistake, and as soon as I can get it corrected, they can do whatever they damned well please."

He eyed my wrath with wistful compassion. "You know, Mole, I wish you'd move back in with us. I'd feel much better about you all around."

I shook my head, knowing that in a minute I'd be beginning to cry. "I like my house, Bart."

"Is it all because of Joyce that you won't come back?"

"No," I lied, and dropped my head so he wouldn't see the tears that were inching down my cheeks. I couldn't tell him how desperately I longed to come home again, or how miserable and lonely I really was. Or how profoundly my estrangement from Joyce had affected my life: when our friendship cracked up, the first big fissure had come in the granite solid foundation of my short existence, and everything since had simply served to make the fissure greater.

After he left, I sat there alone in my lonely, large living room and pondered it: first Joyce and Bart marrying—thus depriving me of a brother and a best friend, as surely as if they'd teamed up on me. Oh, I know this outcome was an accident, but wasn't it also an inevitable one? It seemed so to me, considering all the factors. Joyce and I *couldn't* have remained friends, not at our unsure ages. She had to prove herself as a wife, and a girl old enough to prove it. And she was still trying.

Then there were lots of other things I had to get through: my first love affair, my first "affair," and my first "serious affair," to culminate in a broken engagement; all three of which were normal in outline, but absurd and psycho in detail. Then Mother—that was the big thing, the big wedge that had really split the fissure. If only she hadn't had to die! After that everything had been simply awful and was getting worse.

Would I make it? I doubted it. The Beautiful People did not exist; they were all ugly ones in holiday masks. And now even the holiday seemed over, and all the people I knew were going about their businesses of being narrow and tiresome, beaten—not beat—or purely vicious and corrupt, as honestly poisonous as a bottle with a label.

At fourteen, I had once remarked to our Madison Avenue druggist who met me on my bicycle on the way to the park, "Life is so futile, Mr. Smith!" He had thought it cute, and would never let me forget it.

But it seemed I had been right.

Chapter Seventeen

"Are you as pensive as you look?" he said. "Or are you all stirred up by the tragedy of the *Titanic*, being so close to it now, as it were?"

"I saw 'A Night to Remember' on TV," I replied to Shelley Spivak, and tightened my trenchcoat belt. It had been raining when I left home, so I wore that and had tied a scarf over my head.

"You look downright Bohemian," he grinned at me, "all set for a safari into the darkest wilds of the Village."

I laughed at him weakly. Actually, he couldn't have been more accurate. I'd even left the car in the garage and had come over to Macy's by taxi.

We stood in the specified vestibule where he'd asked me to meet him, and Macy customers rushed in and out of the door, looking preoccupied and slightly worried, as all shoppers somehow do, letting down their umbrellas, brushing at their wet hair. Definitely not the Beautiful People, but just people, the inhabitants of the world I must learn to accept.

"Come, now study this memorial," Shelley said to me, his arm taking mine. We moved out of the way of the Macyites, flattened ourselves against the radiator, which was fortunately cold, and silently perused the plaque and poem together. It was my second go round, for though Shelley had arrived precisely on the dot, I had been early. I was too restless to stay at home.

"Now what do you think of it?" He cocked his head at me for an opinion, as if we were two art experts at a vernissage.

"You can't be serious," I said.

"I can be, but I'm not," he said with a fresh grin. "Come on. Where'd you park your little kiddy-car?"

"If you mean my perfectly good automobile, it's at home."

"Don't trust us, do you? And now I suppose the subway's too good for you, and you'll insist on a taxi."

"I'll insist on a bus," I told him lightly. So we went out in the very unpleasant rain, and jammed ourselves into a rush-hour bus, already packed with its full complement, headed downtown.

We were lucky enough to get two of those straps to swing onto, and as close together as we could ever get without being married or taking another rush-hour trip together via the public transportation, we grinned into each other's eyes, rather foolishly, our noses practically rubbing. "I like you, little Chloe Longtree," he said in a softened low voice.

I didn't say a word, but I felt my body responding. Not to his—it was more as if I had been standing at stiff attention for a long time, and suddenly was told to relax. I was almost happy as I held onto my bus strap, idly watching the streets flash by. By flash, I mean all the electrical heralding of the signs on the stores and buildings along the way, for it was almost dark. It was March, and spring was not yet in the air, only sort of behind it, so everything still said Winter! outside, and what was to come was not yet strong enough to make a faint whisper. But those who longed for spring, surely knew it was there. Like a crocus bulb, still brown, but a crocus bulb all the same, and a live one.

As we traveled all the nostalgia I had ever felt for this city traveled through me, as if intravenously injected, and I felt satisfied and warm with it quietly flowing through my veins, nourishing me. I thought of all the nights when Avery and I had sneaked off in Bart's car, that last summer before I was old enough to drive, and how we had toured this grand old town, up one secret street down a familiar one, each different and wonderful, as rich in treasure and terror as an unmined silver lode. And most of it I would never explore, but it was there, all there. Forever, fixed as a star. More enduring than the people who gave it its sparkling highlights. But there were always more people, and there was always New York.

"What are you so quiet for? Are you sad?" Shelley asked me.

"I'm not sad. I was thinking about—things."

"Your husband?"

I gave him a startled look. "No," I said.

"Avery told me about him."

"I gathered."

"Want to talk?"

"Not on a bus," I answered, then added, "or actually

anywhere." And I didn't. I had sealed Pritch up in my mind, walled him up as surely as if I'd used mortar and trowel to do it, and only occasional chinks opened up—such as Bart's enlightening information about Pritch and Lesley this afternoon. These I closed up as quickly as possible. I didn't want or need any chinks. Pritch was buried and finished.

Shelley helped me off the bus, handing me down as if I were something precious and fragile. "We've got a long hike from here," he said. "We could take a cab."

"Let's hike," I said, even though the rain was harder than ever and I knew it would wash my face clean of every vestige of makeup, until I looked like one of those ancient Greek statues, eyeless and colorless without their polychrome. However, I didn't care. Shelley was one of those men with whom it wouldn't matter: he liked me for myself. Anyway, I found myself thinking, what did it matter to me what Shelley Spivak thought? He was just a nice, rather rough joe who was befriending me. I didn't ask myself why, but it did occur to me to inquire as to how he got the name Shelley.

"Used to write poetry—as I told you," he said with his almost shy sidewise grin—the grin that must have endeared a great many women to him; it was terribly incongruous with the rest of his rather bold personality. "My Hebrew name sounds a little like Shelley, so it was an easy transition. My family is orthodox. They live in Denver. In a section so Jewish that it's like a ghetto. Only my old man is in the jewelry business and has got lots of money. They have a big house— a cook and a maid."

"Why do you keep saying 'they'?" I asked him.

"Because it is 'they.' I don't live there. Don't care for my stepmother." He grinned again. "Don't care for the whole set-up. I haven't been to synagogue since—oh, since I was bar-mitzvahed."

Then he explained that bar-mitzvah was sort of the equivalent of Catholic confirmation, about which I didn't know too much either. He looked at me. "We're worlds apart, Chloe Longtree, but I like you. And we dig each other. As if we were long-lost relatives. Maybe you *are* from one of the lost tribes of Israel. With a name like Longtree—you sure it wasn't Grossbaum once upon a time?"

I laughed at him, but I'll have to admit I felt what he felt: I hadn't been so close to anybody for a long time. He was like Bart in another guise, and yet curiously like Pritch too, all the men I'd ever cared about, but with a difference. When he took my hand, and held it as we walked along, nothing could have been righter, more warm, more secure.

After a while he said, "What's the score with this old man of yours?"

"Who?"

"Your man," he said, laughing lightly. "This cat you're married to. Love him?"

I confessed I didn't know, was hopelessly awash and confused by everything. He listened carefully. "What you need is a good Alabama divorce. You've got to wipe the slate clean, kid. Can't afford to make too many mistakes at your age."

"I've already made them," I said, and told him more. Before I'd finished, I'd outlined my whole life's history for him.

He appeared thoughtful as we plodded through the rain.

"Maybe you ought to hit bottom," he said at last. "It can't hurt a girl like you. You're the kind who has to find out how the other half lives before you can live your half."

"Sounds frightful." I tried to laugh.

"No, seriously. I mean it." He put his hand on my shoulders and turned me toward the street light to look into my wet and probably expressionless face. "A girl like you only grows up by growing."

"I'm growing," I said.

"Are you?" he asked in that crisp, challenging tone of his. "I don't think so, really. It's mostly vicarious—like wading in and lifting your friend Avery out of hot water. You only get wet, not scalded. You think you learn from that?"

"I hope so," I said.

"You afraid to get your head soaked?"

"No, not really. I just don't think it's necessary."

"Then why does your instinct keep sending you back for more?"

"My instinct?" I said, truly puzzled.

"Yes. You wander from one steam bath to another. Isn't it time you sat down in one to see what it's like?"

"What do you suggest?"

Still holding me by the shoulders, he gazed at my face. "This may rock you," he said slowly, "but shack up with me—not in that fancy, self-indulgent pad of yours uptown, but down here—cold-water flat, where you learn how to cook and wait on me and do all the things a woman of mine would do. You game?"

It *did* rock me. "I'm not sure—"

"Then you're chicken. You're scared."

"It isn't that. It's just that—" How could I tell him? How could I say that I didn't think I wanted to be "his woman"? Shelley was my brother. "It would be a little like incest at this point," I said.

"Oh, I see," he said slowly, releasing my shoulders. "I've involved you in the brotherhood bit. Well, we'll see what we can do about that. How's this?"

Before I knew it, Shelley had reached up around my waist, had pulled me to him and was kissing me—a long kiss, full of love and passion. "You ever been kissed like that, kid?" he asked, his voice as husky as my own suddenly felt.

"No," I said under my breath. "I haven't."

Then we started walking on again, as naturally as if nothing had happened. But something had, and I knew as soon as we hit Seymour Marlboro's lair something more was going to happen.

If I were Avery's guardian angel, I was also a fallen one.

Chapter Eighteen

Sy's apartment was a walk-up on a street called Greenwich Street; it was lined with other tenements, all dark and
condemned looking, a few new or remodeled apartment
houses which undoubtedly charged exorbitant rents and
caught only the most desperate or naive of tenants intent
upon having a Village residence; and then there were a lot of
turn-of-the-century places of business and warehouses. An
ominous locale, at best, and I was thoroughly glad I was not
alone. Moreover, I was a million times better than not alone:
I was with one of the most exciting—or *the* most exciting
person I'd ever met. Every casual touch was like a caress;
whether he brushed my arm opening the door for me, or
took my hand to help me, or just looked at me; with Shelley
a look was a touch, a vital physical contact.

We climbed the stairs to Seymour's "pad," I, feeling very
tired and wet, yet steaming with warmth as if I sat before an
open fire, and somehow sleepily immune to all the bleak aw-
fulness of the tenement house, all because I knew Shelley was
right behind me.

He knocked at the door. With a one-two, one-two-three
knock that was like a password of identification. Seymour

opened the door just a crack, and peered at us skeptically.

Shelley pushed open the door. "Hi, Sy. This is Chloe here. She came down to view her side-kick."

"What?" asked Seymour vaguely, not yet willing to part with his hold on the door, but he had really been brushed aside, and Shelley was striding in. That's the only word for the way he walked, entered or left a place, striding—as if it were a form of travel that could take prizes, like track-running; he did it proudly and well.

I sort of crept in behind him. There were two or three strangers in this strange room, all huddled together, frightened and hostile looking, their eyes big in sunken faces, their clothes as nondescript as a bag of rags. But then the light was bad, admittedly.

"Where's Avery?" Shelley asked with authority, looking around, his hands still in his raincoat pockets. He was rather like a private eye.

"Asleep," Sy gestured toward a closed door. "You want a stick?" he added. "We're all turned on."

"Sure," said Shelley easily. "Pack us a lunch."

"Her too?" Sy said with a gesture toward me.

"Sure," Shelley said in the same easy tone. "She's with it."

I looked at him, much as a child does toward a parent in a roomful of strange people, but by the back of his raincoat, I could tell he had thrown me into this pool on my own, sink or swim. He expected me to swim.

Very timorously, I moved over to the far side of the room, near the huddle of others, near the bookcases made out of orange crates, the only illumination coming from candles stuck in empty chianti bottles, much tallow-encrusted, with variegated colors. The furniture was equally modestly immodest; it all looked as if it had been picked up from a garbage heap—a sagging double bed on one wall with a musty, worn velvet cover, the color gone back to brown from whatever it had been, like seared winter grass; a few canvases on the wall, all very vividly violent in stroke and color, unframed, of course, still on stretchers, and in one corner a huge old upholstered chair, obviously a street relic, which done over, would have screamed for room and air even in the Allyn's old fortress uptown.

"You don't like it, I see," Seymour said in a surly way, obviously having followed my glance around his place.

"I like it fine," I said quietly, and pointedly looked toward his three pale-faced friends he hadn't bothered to introduce. He still didn't.

"I'm Marjorie," said one.

"The name's Rudy," said the male of the trio, getting to his feet in a wobbly way, "and that's Sonya, only I don't think she's up to getting up. Say hello, Sonya."

A weak hand was raised, and then let to fall like a withered blossom, or a tired flag, and Sonya's wide open eyes gazed on at me unseeingly.

I felt a cigarette being put into my hand. "Smoke deep," came Shelley's voice.

I felt myself being pushed down on the cruddy velvet bed. Shelley's arm was behind me, supporting me. He still had his coat on, as I did. "Where's Avery?" I asked after a deep puff. It tasted like burning grass.

"She's asleep inside. Like I told you," I heard Seymour saying petulantly. "If you don't believe me, go see."

"I will," I said getting to my feet, slightly staggering. I thought I was just off balance, but maybe those two puffs had had their effect. Anyway, holding the cigarette, and puffing on it, deeply, as I had been instructed, I went toward the closed door.

"Doesn't she know how much joints cost?" I heard Seymour say. "She's smoking it like a Chesterfield."

"She'll learn," was Shelley's answer. "Anyway, she's got enough to buy and sell S.K.S."

I tried to think about that, steadily, sensibly, as I pushed opened the bedroom door, but even then I knew it was a postponed topic: I'd smoked that stick of marijuana too faithfully following the laid-down rules, and I was as high as a kite; no better, no worse than the others. My mind was as blurred as a spoiled water color, and I didn't care, I didn't care....

When I came to, I was obviously in bed, and the first thing I saw was the hem of the bedsheet; it was clammy and dirty, and in my face. I looked around. The one window I saw streamed dirty, mottled light, because the window was that way in addition to being cracked and uncurtained. I turned my head. There his head lay on the other dirty pillow. It was a sleeping face, very oily looking but beautiful, dark as my own was fair, and very peaceful. Then I knew what warm band encircled my waist: his arm. I stirred away from it, and it tightened. "My love," came the murmur from his sleep. "My love."

Then he was awake, and his face was upon mine, as it had been in the bus, but with all the ardor of possession, and his naked body moved to the top of mine, also naked, and he had me clamped down in a togetherness that *McCall's* talks about, but may or may not mean....

And when it was all over, he said, "You are my real wife. You're the only one. Don't you feel that, Chloe? Don't you?"

And I did. The way Shelley made love to me was a fulfillment. And I belonged to him. As he had predicted, I was his woman. I knew that no matter what ever happened to us, I was his woman. "Where are we?" I finally managed to ask.

"My place," he said. "Fourth Avenue. A real dump."

"Where's Avery?" I asked, feeling as tremulous as I sounded. I had let her down. I had come to save her, and look at me.

"She's okay. Or at least she was. She's still at Sy's place. Out. Like a light. Like you were. You two were gabbing for hours and I kept bringing you sticks, then you both went. Just like that."

"It's worse than liquor," I said.

"It's better. It's clean," he corrected me. "You said a lot of very smart things—to all of us—before you passed out. Don't you remember?"

"No," I said, wanting very much, all of a sudden, to be home in my own bed. "I don't remember anything. I blacked out."

"Sounds like sauce, but it was pot, all the same. Maybe

you're a doll who can't take it."

"No, I don't think I can," I said, rising to an elbow, pre-paratory to going home.

"Come here," he said hoarsely, drawing me back down beside him.

After a while we lay back, watching the dawn through the cracked windows, over the moldy sheets and scratchy Army blankets, and I told him all this. I told him about Pritch and the way *he* made love; I told him about my ex-fiancée, Charles La Marr; I told him about the casual ones in England. In fact, I told him. I filled in all of the outline I had told him earlier in the night in the rain.

And he told me: about the two wives, the four children. How responsibly unresponsible he felt. "You will marry me, Chloe," he said urgently, but quietly.

"Of course I will," I answered, feeling lightheaded, but very sure of what I was saying. "I've never met anyone like you. But you will take care of me?"

"Always," he promised. "But you know you've got to do a lot of shifting and changing to stand me."

"Such as?"

"I'm not going to be a provider. It's your money."

I shrugged. "It's there."

"And I won't 'belong' you know."

"I don't either," I whispered tiredly, tenderly. And fell asleep.

When I woke up, I looked at my watch which had obvi-ously stopped, and looked around for Shelley. He was in the kitchen part of this strange dwelling, making coffee. Watching for it to boil. It was a strange place, even worse than Seymour's and I sat up, knowing how cold it was, that the gas stove was the only heat, clutching the blanket around my nakedness. "Where's Avery?" I said rather idiotically. And he came over, sat on the bed, tucking the blanket lovingly around my feet.

"Avery's with her man and you are with yours," he said, and then he kissed me.

I shuddered a little, cried, as he pressed me close to him. "I've never felt this way before about anybody, Chloe!" he said in my ear, and his strong arms were around me, placing me just so, and his body merged with mine, and I closed my eyes....

I woke up the next time when it was dark. There was cracked light coming through the cracked window, irregular and vaguely alarming. I touched my foot to his leg. I knew it so well now, and my toe lingered caressingly. He stirred, said "hmmm?" and I asked him to tell me the time, the day, the place.

He gave a deep sigh, and flopped over on his lovely stomach. "Don't know," he breathed, and went off.

I prodded him. "I've *got* to know." I said, thinking of Tennie and Jess. "They'll be out of their minds."

"Who?" he asked sleepily.

I told him, and he sighed again, and started to go back to sleep. "Tell you later."

"No!" I exclaimed, shaking him. "I've got to go home,

Pritch!"

"Pritch!" he answered, sitting straight up in bed and wide awake. He gazed at me, his face full of resentment, almost hatred. "Pritch, is it?"

"I'm sorry, darling," I made an appeal, putting my arms around him. And I was sorry and shocked, by my Freudian slip.

"Come on," he said abruptly, throwing the covers back. "I'm taking you home."

Chapter Nineteen

Shelley refused to come in with me; in fact, he would not even walk me back to the courtyard; just stayed in the taxi. "Good-bye," he said sullenly, seeing me out. "See you around."

"Come in," I pleaded at the point of tears.

He behaved as if he hadn't heard me; and the taxi drove off, at his bidding, while I still stood there, my hand practically still on the taxi door.

There was nothing to do, but go inside. I still had my trenchcoat, thank God, which covered the fact that I had lost my skirt, and wore only my slip and sweater underneath. I felt awful. Here I was, trudging home after—how many days? Without Avery, without wits, in fact as empty as an old beer bottle up for refund. My pocketbook was, I knew, empty as far as money went, but I hopefully felt for my keys. Yes, they were still there. I put them in the lock, turned them, and let myself into the warmly lighted hall. It hadn't changed; not one bit, and when I went into the living room, there sat Avery on the couch, one foot tucked up under her, her hands scratching her hair as it always did when she read, her nose deep into an issue of *The New Yorker.* I just stood, as one returned from the grave, and when she looked up, casually at first, her expression changed to one of horrified surprise, to match my own. "Darling!" she gasped, and we were clutching each other, feeling each other to see if we were real.

About that time Tennie came into the living room, with things on a tray, and she clutched at me and cried, pushed me away and then drew me back, unable to make up her mind whether to kiss me or kill me. "You're just like your mother, Miss Chloe," she said in a truly heartrending way. "I doesn't know whether to whip you or hug you to death!" Thank God, she had the good sense, having been my Mother's watchdog, not to ask me where I'd been. I got rid of her by saying I was hungry.

When she had gone, I looked at Avery—deeply, searchingly, as if a look would tell me more than any conversation possibly could. She was examining me in the same way. Then she broke into one her peals of delighted laughter. "What fools we are! Man, what fools!"

"When did you get here?" I whispered conspiratorially, and she gave me all the data, keeping her voice as low as mine.

"I really can't stand that Sy," she said. "He's the end. Must have been the pot. He's stupid, has bad breath—*and* B.O., even after a nice bath in that lovely tub in his lovely kitchen. We both had one—together, I mean. How could I do it, Chloe? How could I?" Her eyes twinkled as if she were highly pleased about the whole thing. "Well, at least it's over.

I've had my spree—and I *didn't* lose my job. Marvelous Tennie. Told them the most marvelous lie when they called up. But she was frantic, sweetie. Three days *is* a long time—"

"She didn't call Bart, did she?" I asked truly alarmed.

"I'm afraid she did, sweetie. But *I* told him a good lie…just now. He just called a moment ago, for the God knows how manyeth time."

"Oh, my God!" I said, sunk.

"Don't worry. The whole thing's over and done with …just as long as we never see those characters again.…"

I looked at her slowly. How could I tell her I had to see mine again, whether he wanted to see me or not? "What did you think of mine?" I asked her, for a beginning.

Avery laughed. "I wouldn't know him from mine. I was that blasted."

I regarded her gloomily. Lucky Avery! And Shelley had said I was the one who could take it or leave it, snap back.

"Well," she said, getting to her feet, yawning. "Enough of this lovemaking. I've got to get to the office. Do I look pale enough?"

"Too pale," I replied, and asked her what time it was anyway. I learned it was breakfast time.

"You don't look too red-blooded yourself," she said giving me the critical eye. "You must have really lived it up."

"I don't know what you'd call it," I said dully.

"Well, take heart in any case, darling. It really is all over."

Is it? I asked myself, watching her idly as she walked around the room, collecting her cigarettes and things and stuffing them in her purse. She picked up an old hat of mine, looked at it from a couple of angles, and said, "Not bad. Think I'll wear it," and jammed it down on her head. Oddly enough, it looked very chic. But Avery has one of those hat heads. "What are you mooning about?" she asked, giving me a sudden look. "You aren't still high, are you?"

I shook my head, heard her say good-bye, and listened for the door to slam and lock me in, closet me with my thoughts. They were running wild as horses on the range; it seemed a hopeless task to try to catch them. But I had to, and I hoped Tennie would leave me alone for a while. I didn't want any private words with her.

To forestall any, I decided to go up to my room and lie down. I felt terrible. In the physical sense I felt so awful that my mind had almost literally vacated my ruined body, like an astral spirit. But my mind was a sick thing too, trotting up and down hyena-fashion, longing, actually, to be put out of its misery. But the only way short of dying was sleep, and that was impossible.

I lay on the chaise longue and wished for the energy to get up and find some pillows. Instead I used my arms behind my head as cushions. After a while they, at least, went to sleep and when they started to tingle, I had to move them. Another terrific effort, and I doubted if they were worth it. Tennie was tapping at the door as if I were in an infirmary.

"Come on in!" I called rather harshly, and she brought in my breakfast tray, looking subdued but pleased, as if everything were all right again with the world now that I had come home. I could tell she wanted to talk, but I waved her out, saying I was sleepy.

"If you don't watch out, Miss You," she gave me one parting shot from the door, "you gonna end up in a fix."

Gimme one! was the only rejoinder I could think of, and as it was too obscure as far as Tennie was concerned, I didn't use it. But I went on thinking it.

Yes, I certainly needed something to get me out of this one. I couldn't believe it. In the first place, why had I made that silly slip and called him Pritch? Did Shelley and Pritch sound alike? No! Did they look alike, or remind me of each other in any way? No, no, no! But why had he become so infuriated? How could anybody be so contemptibly conceited as to be really upset by a little thing like that? Would I have minded if he had called me Dorothy, or Peggy, or whatever his wives' names were? No, of course not.

I got up and paced around, convincing myself what a good, kind, reasonable, lenient, understanding girl I was. And he was an oaf and a bastard. Uncouth, ugly, smug. It was a good thing it was all over. Avery was right: it had simply been a spree.

This squared away, I decided to go further with the guilt-eradicating, and went and drew myself a bath. I put out my clothes, feeling very luxurious, slightly heady with release. I was back in the scrubbed, scented, comfortable arms of Mother Normality, and no more would I stray. But even as I lowered myself in the tub, I heard the phone ringing, and my heart leaped up like a rainbow trout. I listened alertly, but could hear nothing, of course, for Tennie had taken the call in the kitchen, or wherever she was. And she wouldn't disturb me since she thought I was asleep.

I splashed through that bath as if I were drowning in it and couldn't wait to get to dry land. I dashed to my room and buzzed her on the intercom. "Who was it?" I shouted.

"The cleaners. They done lost your new slipcovers."

I rang off and wearily started to dress. Dress for what? I hadn't the faintest idea. Maybe lunch with Bart was in order, but I couldn't face him yet. And if he called up, worried as hell, to ask me, I'd put him off with some excuse. In point of fact, all I wanted to do was run back to Shelley.

Having admitted it, I dressed as though the house were on fire, thinking as I rushed into my clothes that I didn't even know his address, and would have to go by instinct in order to find his house. But I didn't care, I didn't care! I'd comb Fourth Avenue, look in every house, until I found where Shelley was. I'd find him and make him take me.

When the phone rang, I didn't bother to pick it up, even to listen in to see who it was. Something just told me it wouldn't be Shelley, and whoever it was, it didn't matter. Then I heard Tennie urgently buzz the intercom.

"Who is it?" I cried impatiently.

"It's *him*," she said significantly.

"Who?"

"Mr. Allyn."

"Mr. Allyn?" I echoed stupidly and sat down quite faint on the bed. Slowly I answered the phone.

"Hello, there," Pritch's voice came over the wire, as casual as if he'd seen me an hour before. "Doing anything for lunch?"

In a daze, I heard myself saying no, and agreeing to meet

him at the Ritz in half an hour. As soon as I hung up the phone, I went downstairs and had two straight shots of Bourbon. Tennie looked at me expectantly, eagerly, and I simply closed my eyes and shook my head at her.

I also drove in something of a stupor, ran two red lights, and nearly bumped into a car ahead which made an abrupt and unforgivable stop. I said so too, leaning out of my window and yelling like a truck driver. The man appeared very startled, and I whipped around him smartly and drove away before he could recover himself.

That's how I felt—all crazy.

"You're looking well," Pritch said, giving me an admiring look as he came forward to meet me.

I murmured that he was too, but to tell the truth I was almost in a state of shock, so I hardly saw him.

"I believe our table is ready," he said, wasting no time, and we worked our way back to where our table waited for us.

He immediately set about the business of ordering, explaining to me over the top of the menu that he was very hungry and hoped I was. I said I'd like a drink.

At this, he coolly summoned the waiter and ordered two whiskey sours—what we used to drink together always. I knew life was coming back when it flashed through my wicked mind that his mother would have a fit if she knew he was lunching in this posh place, and drinking liquor to boot. But I said nothing, merely glanced demurely at the napkin in my lap and wondered why I couldn't work up any specific feeling toward him. There should have been love or hate; instead there was a sort of embalmed feeling of tiredness, such as one has when lunching with an old friend who is avoided successfully except two or three times a year. Maybe, I told myself, this will pass, and I put up a warning sign in my mind to watch out for any change.

Lunch ordered, he gave me a long, fond smile. "Well, Chloe," he said, "I'll come to the point at once: now that you have finally given me adequate and acceptable grounds for it, I want a divorce. If you don't get it, I will."

Chapter Twenty

In the same good-natured and breezy manner, he elaborated on how he had had the good fortune to establish these grounds. "You and your pal Avery evidently forgot that Seymour Marlboro was very much in my debt," he explained.

All this news had momentarily deprived me of the powers of speech. Was he trying to say it was all a frame, that I had deliberately walked into a vice-trap Seymour—and apparently Shelley—had laid for me? But I couldn't ask him.

He, however, was continuing quite blithely on his own. Obviously, he didn't need my reply to anything, and went along as if he were giving a memorized speech, one he enjoyed very much.

"—Seymour phoned the good news this morning—that you and his pal Spivak had been couched together, shall we say, for upwards of three days. And of course I know all about that little orgy den run by that fellow Summers, or Saunders, who thinks he is practicing a new form of religion—"

"—I didn't—" I tried to protest, but he took the words out of my mouth.

"—Oh, I know you didn't. But who would believe it in

court? You see, I have you coming and going for adultery. So are you going to be a nice girl and go get yourself a nice quiet divorce, or shall I get a big noisy one?"

"Suit yourself," I said coldly, starting to get up from the table. Then I looked at him. He wore the most odious grin, and the lights flashing in his eyes weren't "angry sea," but typhoon; I had never thought that blue eyes could look tawny, but they did: wild-animal tawny.

I gazed at him somewhat wistfully, as if I were looking over the edge of a precipice toward which I must go, there being no turning back. Why, why? What had changed him? What had cooled passion into pity, then pity into irritable indifference—and now this? "Why do you hate me?" I asked, falteringly.

"Hate you?" His eyes gleamed with triumph again. "I don't hate you. I despise you," his lip positively curled, movie fashion. "Why do you think I walked out on you, because I was 'influenced by my family'?" He gave a laugh like a howl. "I didn't need them to tell me what you were trying to do to me. You and your 'plans'! I was sick of the sight of you long before we even married, and I just went through with it because I thought it was the only thing to do—"

I heard him wearily. "You're very sick, Pritch," I said.

"I'm going to be a lot better from now on!" He said vehemently. "Are you going?" I was still leaning on the table. "If so, go on. All I want to see of you is your signature on divorce papers."

I changed my mind and sat down again. "Let's get this straight," I began. I wanted to hear him say—actually say—

he'd never loved me; but I couldn't put it that way. It was too bare and I was too vulnerable. "You didn't really *have* to marry me, you know, Pritch."

"I know, I know," he waved this aside in annoyance. "The actual invitation was my mistake. I was confused. Lesley and I weren't getting on too well, and I thought of you back in London, and it seemed such a peaceful, pleasant—" He broke off. "—But all that's over and done with. So I made a mistake—one mistake—you made all the rest!"

"Did I?" I asked. "Why didn't you tell me all this when you first felt your fad for me fading? I would have divorced you any time, and gladly."

He threw back his head and simply roared with laughter so raucous and eerie that several people nearby looked uncomfortable and were evidently interrupted in their own conversations. Then he stopped this insane humor. "You know damned well you pulled out every stop to get your way with me," he accused me.

I looked down at my untouched drink, rubbed my finger around the bottom of the glass. I wanted to say: I thought you felt the same for me. I looked up. Hadn't he? A scowl stood in his eyes. No. You can never look at a person like that if you have once loved them. He had been selling himself a bill of goods, that was all—me. He had made a manly unheartfelt effort, and so naturally now he despised me, just as he despised himself. I had been right in the first place: he couldn't love. Only maybe his awful family he pretended to hate.

I stood up again, this time for good. "All I can say, Pritch, is that you're brainwashed to tatters. When you're not busy laundering your own deformed mind, you let others have a try. Better try a prefrontal lobotomy."

This was mean, but more than the essence of truth was there: Brother Allyn was the last person on earth to know his own mind. It would be a challenge to anybody. "Good-bye," I said under my breath.

I walked away briskly, trying to feel imperious, and the speech he barked after me didn't hurt: "See to it you get that divorce and quick about it!" It simply served to inform anyone around who had failed to catch the drift earlier that we were having a final marital scene.

As I opened the phone booth, I had that deadened but composed feeling of a wronged person. His venom had acted as a cathartic; I was purified, young, blameless. Therefore, my voice was small when I called Bart and told him what had happened. He was mystified to hear of Pritch's insulting behavior, his lightning quick reappearance, his sudden insistence on a divorce. He wanted to know if I had done something to bring it about? I vigorously denied that I had—for in a way I hadn't. It had all been so indirect. The lawyer was less subtle in his suggestions that I had done something to precipitate it, or to "give him a chance to pounce, show his true colors." Both Bart and the lawyer missed the fine points involved, so it seemed to me: that I had been an innocent, trusting wife, waiting for my husband. *I* had not resorted to spying and other low tricks. It was frustrating not to be able to point this out, but I felt I had to tie my own tongue. It would not do to tell either that Pritch had gotten the "goods" on me, and had long been waiting for them. My lawyer, an old and experienced hand at the game, merely sighed, probably quite aware of my small deceit, and advised me, since I said I no longer cared to have Pritch back, to plan to divorce him as quickly as possible.

I said I would, and knew then, firmly, I really wanted to.

It was clear that Pritch had gone quite mad, so mad that all the things he had said were unbelievable. How had he been able to accumulate that fine backlog of hatred out of midair? Even granted that his family helped him assiduously, and that Joyce and possibly Lesley had done their share. Where had it come from if not from insanity? It was so unjust and untrue that it didn't touch me. All those months of fidelity, waiting for him to come back, yearning for him…and he was just waiting for me to fall into a trap. Or had he imagined that too? That Seymour had played hand and glove with him? If so, what had prevented Seymour from telephoning me and arranging a meeting instead of waiting for a chance encounter? It didn't make any sense at all. I was almost tempted to call Pritch's mother and have a long talk with her—if she'd let me—but that was foolish. If he'd made all this up, she wouldn't know what I was talking about, and if he hadn't, then she wouldn't talk to me in the first place.

Thoughtfully, I drove back home; Bart said he would meet me there and we would talk about everything and what the best course was. I debated telling him the whole thing. But it would have terrible repercussions if I did: he would immediately insist, for instance, that I rid myself forever of Avery; would blame it all on her bad influence. Then, also, he would probably take steps to see to it that no more Shelley Spivaks crossed my doorstep for a long time to come. And I wanted Shelley Spivak to cross my doorstep; to cross it and recross it, to camp on it, to carry me over it. I didn't believe for an instant that he had been any party to Pritch's ugly little scheme with Seymour—and I even doubted if dumb Seymour had done more than just shoot off his mouth inopportunely and after the fact. Pritch's story was all too much of a fantasy, something invented to hide hurt pride, probably, when Seymour told him about Shelley and me. But damn Seymour anyway! And Avery had said it was all over, just a harmless spree....

Bart gave me what I can only describe as a lot of stern sympathy which turned out to be quite boring as he had nothing new to add, being ignorant of some of the developments. And when I tried to describe Pritch's behavior, deleting, of course, all of the salient items, such as *why* he was so insistent now on a divorce, Bart gave me a very doubtful look, and I knew he thought I was exaggerating. But his overall theme, the one that ran in and out of our conversation like a fugue, was his plea to come "back home."

But I was as determined as he was. "Come back now and fall over Lesley and Pritch too, probably?"

Bart violently insisted this wouldn't happen, but I shook my head. "You never know." And since Lesley was Joyce's sister, he had to admit there was some truth in what I said.

I guess Bart saw my impatience, though he had none himself, and stood up quite reluctantly to leave. "I have a bad feeling about all this, Mole," he lingered at the door to say.

And gave me a queer look, as if he were tempted to say something more—like how he sensed I was holding out on him, or something. Then he gazed at me with a long look, as if he were trying to memorize my face.

Finally, I got rid of him by promising to come to dinner next week, a duty I'd successfully avoided for months.

As soon as he left, I left, and I found I was so nervous I could hardly drive. Every stoplight made me want to scream with impatience, and the traffic moved at the pace of a funeral march all the way downtown.

Once on Fourth Avenue, I frantically searched the buildings for some landmark. Then the old unconscious decided to stop being so selfish, and up popped the memory that his house had been vaguely in the vicinity of the secondhand-book section. This narrowed it down considerably, and I only had to drive up and down those few blocks three times before I spotted the house. I jumped out of the car, parking it illegally and not caring a bit, and rushed into the house.

I panted up the grimy old stairs, creaking as if they were in pain because of being walked on. It was up near the top, I remembered that. Maybe the fourth floor? I stopped to get my bearings and tried the door to the left. It seemed the right one.

At first my knocks were merely businesslike, then, I'm afraid, I more or less pounded, and then to my astonishment, and probably because I had been so rough with it, the old door sprang open, as if giving up before superior odds. I pushed it in a little further and gazed at the place, the late scene of my lovely crime. Quite clearly, no one was at home.

I took a few trial steps, wondering as I did so how Shelley could bear to live in such filth and poverty. Then it came to me with overwhelming certainty that he didn't—maybe never had. Hurriedly, I walked around the two rooms, searching for some sign of him—books, clothes, anything. There was nothing. Either this was an apartment (if one could call it that) borrowed especially for assignations, or else he had moved, and in a great hurry too. I was reduced to a thousand shards by this realization, and walked out of the place like the sole survivor of a building just bombed.

I trudged back to the car and just sat in it, slumped over the wheel. I kept urging myself to cry, cry, but I couldn't cry, and as so often happens in times of great stress—at least with me—a crazy tune came into my head, and I found myself humming it aloud; without being able to identify it, naturally, this being my day for total frustration.

You can't sit here all night, were the words I finally managed to fit to the tune, since they were so apt, but I still sat there all the same. At last, I started the car, and drove back uptown at the funereal pace I had encountered coming down, only I set this one for myself, much to the exasperation of end-of-the-day drivers, anxious to get home. But I was oblivious to them, oblivious to such a degree that I was almost blissful, still humming to myself, daft as Ophelia. Once or twice the thought of Avery crossed my mind, but she disappeared along with other scudding clouds of thought. Maybe if I called her, she'd have some practical suggestions. But why bother?

At the garage, the man asked me if I'd be needing the car

anymore that night, and I told him no in such a dim happy voice that I'm sure he thought I'd just come from the dentist where I'd been given gas. I sauntered along the street, humming still, and laughing out loud every now and then for it seemed—my entire life, I mean—such a hugely preposterous dirty joke. Lucky Chloe Longtree became my new cry, and I chanted it out loud every now and then, just for laughs. I met a few people who turned full around in the street to stare, but for the most part, this being New York, I was left to enjoy my madness in private.

It was probably after five when I let myself in the house; or if it wasn't, Avery was home early. For I heard her laughing as I walked through the hall. Then I saw her—saw him. She and Shelley were sitting together on the couch and they both looked up expectantly when I entered.

"Company!" Avery greeted me. Shelley, without getting up, lifted a hand at me and said, "Howdy."

"Howdy," I replied from a previous life, and collapsed in a chair. I guess they just thought I was tired.

Chapter Twenty-One

The instant Avery left the room, Shelley and I were all over each other, as they say. Vulgar as it sounds, I know there is no better way to describe it.

"Darling, darling," he said incessantly as he kissed my eyes, my hair.

When Avery returned, almost inopportunely, she seemed quite amazed to see how close we were. "Well, you two certainly don't believe in letting a second go unoccupied, do you?"

"No, we don't," I told her, turning my head back to Shelley to get kissed some more.

"From now on," he said, "this is a full-time job. I've come to stay."

Avery watched us as we kissed again. "You're kidding, of course," she said after a while.

"No, I'm not," he said quite seriously. "Am I, darling?" he turned to me for corroboration. I looked at him adoringly, scarcely aware of what he wanted me to corroborate.

"But you *can't* live here," Avery said, frowning. "Chloe's lawyer wouldn't allow a man to live in the house until she's divorced."

"Is that true, sweetheart?" he asked me softly.

I considered it I wanted desperately for him to stay. "Maybe we can work it out some way," I replied. "Maybe since Avery is here, she can act as official chaperone. Then of course there are Tennie and Jess—I don't see why it couldn't be done."

"You're both simply crazy!" Avery announced in exasperation. "What if Pritch gets hold of this and wants to make something of it?"

"Pritch has already made something of it," I said carefully and gave them both a full rundown on my non-luncheon luncheon date with him.

Avery couldn't have been more surprised, but Shelley made no comment. Instead, he looked bored, as if he wished we'd hurry and get the whole discussion finished; he kept squeezing my hand, touching my hair, as if anxious to get back to the serious business of semi-private lovemaking. Consequently, the subject was dispatched in short order, leaving Avery far from satisfied with what she heard. I confess I felt a little guilty as I allowed myself to be moved back into the ecstatic circle of Shelley's arms, and I didn't blame Avery for looking on coldly. Presently, she got up and left the room.

When she did this, I broke away from him momentarily. "We really shouldn't, darling. Not in front of her." I whispered to him.

"Why not? She's a big girl. Anyway, she's a third wheel around here."

It shocked me and saddened me, this home truth. I wondered what Shelley and I should do about it.

But Avery evidently recovered her good nature and her poise, for when the three of us went to Grand Central just before dinner, she couldn't have been in better spirits. Both of us twitted Shelley for having checked his luggage in a public locker instead of bringing it directly to the house when he left his Fourth Avenue digs.

"It seemed a wee mite too presumptuous—even for me," he said with his wonderful crooked smile. "How was I to know that Chloe really meant all she said? It's one thing to hope it, and another to know it."

Both of them beamed at me as if I were in a bridal bower, and I beamed back, feeling the same way, but a bit puzzled. I had remembered that Shelley had insisted I come live with him—not the other way around, which I had been prepared to do. Admittedly, however, I found it far more comfortable for him to move uptown. For secretly I knew Pritch had been right in his evaluation of me as a housewife: if I had to rough it, I probably could never make it.

So none of us pursued this subject any further; it was tacitly understood that I had invited Shelley to share my bed and board, just as it was understood that Shelley had preferred my conveniences to his own squalor and misery, forced upon him by lack of funds. I think we all felt relieved, took deep breaths of thanksgiving, and praised providence that I could afford to foot the bills, and thus insure success to our amorous venture. In other words, it was as if I were the rich businessman who finances the brilliant young lad who discovers a gold mine but hasn't the cash to exploit it on his own.

Even Tennie and Jess went along with this to some degree, so cheered were they by the sight of my obvious happiness. At dinner that night, we all behaved like fools—at one minute young children misbehaving at table, and at the next the tender silly young couple, surrounded by doting, approving family. In a spurt of sheer *joie de vivre* at one point I was even sitting in Shelley's lap, my arm lovingly around his neck, eating from his plate, being fed like a pet bird.

After dinner, Avery discreetly said she thought she'd go to a movie. With a pang of guilt, I too readily agreed, betraying my eagerness to be alone with Shelley, but aware at the same time that we were sort of crowding her out of the place where she lived.

"Do you really like him?" I asked in an anxious whisper, seeing her out the door.

She crinkled her eyes a little, getting ready to say something sharp and funny. "He needs a little polishing. Too bad you got the job first!"

I couldn't have been more delighted.

"But," she added, "don't let him make a squaw out of you. It's not your role."

"I won't," I promised, meaning it.

She gave me a little enigmatic smile and left.

Tennie was the next to be heard from. She had brought me her approval and Jess' too, but with provisors attached. "He don't seem much like the rest of your friends," she ventured. "But he looks to be a mighty fine man. Growed up; knows what he's doing and maybe can settle you down some.

But Miss You, it don't seem right he should live here—even with me and Jess and Miss Avery around. Don't you reckon you ought to see what the law says…?"

Reluctantly, I admitted maybe I should. After all, we could be together almost all the time if he actually slept elsewhere; and it wasn't worth it to jeopardize our future. I asked Shelley's opinion; I desperately had to know he understood before I even consulted the lawyer.

He saw it all right away because his mind worked in a flash, like a diamond drill. "Darling, of course!" he agreed. "I was so absorbed in you this afternoon that I wasn't thinking too much about consequences. But if the divorce is on the fire—and the sooner the better for me—we mustn't do anything to impede it."

He got up briskly, started toward his luggage. It nearly broke my heart; my fantasy had been so way ahead of my reason that already I felt divorced, married to him, and settled down into our life together.

"Where will you go?" I cried, as if he were leaving forever.

"A hotel," he said calmly, still smiling.

But he hasn't a soul! hasn't anything except those two pathetic old suitcases! "Wait a minute," I said hurriedly, and went to the desk and wrote a check for him. I pressed it into his hand. "Don't look at it," I begged him. "Just take it. For running expenses."

He looked at it anyway, and gave that low whistle of astonishment I'd heard from him before "You're joking," he said, handing it back. "There isn't that much money."

"There is, there is!" I insisted. "Take it and let's not discuss it at all. It's my fault, not yours, that you have to live elsewhere. Now go on and check in a hotel and come right back."

Which is what he did.

Chapter Twenty-Two

Lingeringly, tenderly, we parted each night after a long, lovely day together, and each time he left, it nearly killed me. The days were spent going places together—hand in hand— places I would have never gone by myself, and with few other people. He was marvelously intelligent, and was as well informed as a quiz show winner about just anything, it seemed to me. There was nothing, apparently, he didn't know, for there seemed to be nothing he hadn't done. He was a gourmet chef, for instance, and Tennie even let him experiment in her kitchen and admitted he'd taught her a thing or two. And his knowledge always came up so casually, in the course of things we did—like the afternoon we went to the Cloisters and looked at the herb garden: he knew the complete culinary and medicinal history of every herb. That was when I found out he liked to cook, and had even worked for a time as a chef at the Waldorf.

He knew about things like hunting too (as well as Hemingway); 10th century music and medieval poetry, falconry, skiing, all the words to Broadway hits, the battles of the Civil War, 19th century bestsellers—*St. Elmo*, for instance—where the highest waterfalls in the world were located, their exact height, all the famous murders in history, the names of the English kings and their houses, who Brenda Frazier had married and when. Ad infinitum. And he could spell too.

We had marvelous times together, but the strain of waiting for the divorce was very hard on both of us. I was on the phone a dozen times a day with my lawyer, trying to speed him up in getting the details arranged. Finally a date was set for my departure—a whole month away.

It was during this period that Shelley began to drink again—hit the sauce, as he called it. He told me he had been on the wagon for years and years, or ever since he had discovered the joys of marijuana. Maybe I'm stuffy, but I absolutely did not want any pot-smoking going on in my house, and while there was no need to tell Shelley, he knew it, and that was why he drank. Consequently, I felt very guilty and responsible for his drinking, and wouldn't have dreamed of criticizing him for it. Avery was the one who pointed out that the liquor bills were simply tremendous; I had preferred to ignore it.

Liquor had an ulterior effect on Shelley's disposition, and I hated to be around him when he was drunk. Although he always apologized for it the next day, and often said he didn't remember anything, he was very surly, and once quite violent: he hurled a lamp at me. After that episode, I realized something had to be done. I asked him why he drank so much.

"To forget," he told me, as if it were an idiotic question, the answer being self-evident.

I didn't then go on to ask him if he was unhappy, for the answer to this indeed did seem self-evident. Something was worrying him terribly.

"Do you need money? Do you have debts?" I asked, hoping I could help.

"I don't inquire into your business," he answered coldly, and looked ready to flare into a rage.

This was all surprising to me; I had thought he had a contemplative disposition.

But the real trouble—not just danger signals—started one afternoon when I came in early, my appointment at the hairdressers' having been canceled, found the living room blue and foggy with marijuana smoke, and confronted not only Shelley very high on pot, but three other men I'd never seen before and trust I'll never have to see again.

They were lounging around, and apparently Shelley had just been reading aloud to them from his favorite poet: Shelley. He was in a dreamy, lovable mood, insisted on pulling me down beside him on the couch and continuing his reading. He didn't even notice that I was stiff as a ramrod within his embrace.

"Baby, baby," he said. "You're my baby. Somebody give little Chloe girl a joint."

I emphatically refused, eyeing the three strangers with open dislike, while they eyed me back, rather covetously. One had teeth like a lycanthrope and long unwashed hair; another was so badly pock-marked that his features themselves seemed to be just further results of his skin trouble; and the third had such shifty eyes that they ran around in his head as if he had no control over them. Maybe it was a nervous tic, but if so I have never seen anyone who more deserved to have this particular disorder.

I stayed just a few seconds, then stood up and quite pointedly announced I was going upstairs. Shelley waved me away casually enough, but less than a half hour later, he lunged into my bedroom and hotly accused me of alienating his friends. "Dirty little snob!" he shouted, then wheeled out and I saw no more of him that day.

All of which made me more and more anxious to leave, get my divorce, and come back to start life all over again. Somehow I thought by wiping the slate clean, removing all the stress, Shelley and I would be happy again. I say Shelley and I because in spite of it all I was happy; though his growing restiveness bothered me, I was still impervious to gloom, being wildly, hedonistically transported with passionate love.

Two days before my departure date, Avery came to me and said, "Do you have any idea what happened to my pearls? They're the only good thing Madre had left to leave me."

I didn't like the suspicious tone of her voice, but tactfully refrained from saying so. Instead, I helped her look for them, but they were gone. And she couldn't remember when she'd seen them last, as she seldom wore them. "Don't worry," I told her. "I'm insured."

"And a good thing too," she muttered under her breath.

"What do you mean by that?" I challenged her.

"Nothing at the moment, but everything at some future date when you're more receptive."

"I'm as receptive as I'll ever be," I informed her in cold resentment.

"Possibly," she commented in a tight-lipped way, and

turned, prepared to let it go at that.

"Listen, say what you have to say now!"

"Not if you ask me in that lovely manner."

"Do say what you want to say," I said, quieter. "I really do want to hear, and I promise I won't protest—no matter what it is."

"All right," she sighed, "but let's sit down for it. This is not going to be easy."

We sat down in her room, which was very sunny and cheerful—in direct contrast to the bleak, solemn looks we exchanged. "Your little friend is a thief," she began.

I rose up in my chair, ready to murder her, but she said, "Remember your promise? Let me say all this, and then if you like, I'll go—anything you wish. I'm still very much your friend, Chloe, no matter what you think." She paused to see if she could risk going on, and though my eyes were blazing, she risked it, thank God.

"If you'll look at your jewel box, I think you'll find it nearly empty. It wasn't my business to look, of course, but when this fell out of his jacket pocket the other day—" she produced a pawn ticket and presented it to me "—I'll admit I sort of snitched it. Sounds like yours, doesn't it?"

I didn't look at it; I couldn't. I simply crumpled it in my hand, feeling as if I were crumpling myself. For of course I knew the ring was gone. And for days I had persuaded myself that I had misplaced it—or tried to persuade myself. Then I heard her go through the rest—all things I knew: the check forgeries (which I had honored), the strange seedy looking visitor with the scraggly beard who slunk around outside in the street every other day or so, pacing up and down furtively, obviously waiting for somebody (I pretended I didn't think he was waiting for Shelley; I pretended I didn't think he was a dope pusher and was in partnership with my love); but the thing she told me I did not know was about his extra-curricular love life. "First," she said evenly, "he made whopping passes at me. I don't know why. Maybe so I wouldn't tattle on him, for he knew from the start I was on to him. But the pay-off came yesterday when Western Union called back to tell Mr. Spivak his message was undelivered. I simply got a copy of the message."

"How?" My voice was faint and distant.

"By telling them I was Mrs. Spivak. They seemed to find this a little odd, and I think you can see why when I read it to you; or better still, read it yourself, if you can read my writing. I took it all down over the phone."

She placed it in my dead hand, and I read it with my dead eyes:

"Mrs. Dorothy Spivak, Fargo Park, California.

Darling, am renting first-rate house for us for two months. Plenty of room for you and Sally and the baby. Will wire you the other $200 and carfare in a few days as soon as bonus check comes through."

"Bonus check," I said lifelessly.

Chapter Twenty-Three

"People have had nervous breakdowns over less," Avery said gently.

I agreed, but didn't feel up to nodding. Instead, I stared at the sunbursts in the clouds we were passing through. It was wonderful flying weather, and aside from feeling a little weak from having been in bed for two weeks with what everyone agreed was psychosomatic pneumonia, I felt calm if not serene; very glad to be on my way to Reno at last; very glad to have Avery going with me.

There had been no trouble excising Shelley. I simply casually sat him down, with Bart, Avery, my lawyer and Tennie as witnesses, and told him what I knew. And at the end of my speech, he gave me his funny, charming little smile and said, "Touché," and went to the door, saluting us as he left, grand to the end.

"You'll probably have dope addicts and pushers knocking on your door for years," Avery said conversationally.

"No, I won't," I assured her. "Somebody else may have. But I'm selling the house."

"Why didn't you tell me?"

"I just decided, just now," I told her with a grin.

"Then what?"

"The European bit again, I guess," I sighed. "After all, one Beautiful People came out of it, even if he did turn out to be a hideosity with a strong case of insanity."

"You and your damned Beautiful People!" she chided me. "Honestly, Chloe, I'd think you would have had enough by now. Can't you settle for just People? I get into scrapes— but nothing like yours. What's the matter with you, are you oversexed or something?"

"Probably," I said. "I may give myself a nice hysterectomy for Christmas."

She giggled violently. "You're the end!" she exclaimed.

And I thought to myself that I might very well be.